Meet the staff of
THE TREEHOUSE TIMES

AMY—The neighborhood newpaper is Amy's most brilliant idea ever—a perfect project for her and her friends, with a perfect office location—the treehouse in Amy's backyard!

ERIN—A great athlete despite her tiny size, Erin will be a natural when it comes to covering any sports-related story in the town of Kirkridge.

LEAH—Tall and thin with long, dark hair and blue eyes, Leah is the artistic-type. She hates drawing attention to herself, but with her fashion-model looks, it's impossible not to.

ROBIN—With her bright red hair, freckles and green eyes, and a loud chirpy voice, nobody can miss Robin—and Robin misses nothing when it comes to getting a good story.

Keep Your Nose in the News with
THE TREEHOUSE TIMES Series
by Page McBrier

(#1) UNDER 12 NOT ALLOWED

Coming Soon

(#3) SPAGHETTI BREATH
(#4) FIRST COURSE: TROUBLE
(#5) DAPHNE TAKES CHARGE

PAGE McBRIER grew up in Indianapolis, Indiana, and St. Louis, Missouri, in a large family with lots of pets. In college she studied children's theater and later taught drama in California and New York. She currently lives in Rowayton, Connecticut, with her husband, Peter Morrison, a film producer, and their two small sons.

THE TREEHOUSE TIMES #2

The Kickball Crisis

Page McBrier

AN AVON CAMELOT BOOK

THE TREEHOUSE TIMES #2: THE KICKBALL CRISIS is an original publication of Avon Books. This work has never before appeared in book form.

AVON BOOKS
A division of
The Hearst Corporation
105 Madison Avenue
New York, New York 10016

First Avon Camelot Printing: October 1989

CAMELOT TRADEMARK REG. U.S. PAT. OFF. AND IN OTHER COUNTRIES. MARCA
REGISTRADA, HECHO EN U.S.A.

Printed in the U.S.A.

OPM   10   9   8   7   6   5   4   3   2

To Susan Cohen,
with gratitude

THE TREEHOUSE TIMES

#2

The Kickball Crisis

Chapter One

"Do you think it's possible to put a heater up here?" asked Robin Ryan. She stared at the little puffs of fog her breath made in the cold air. "I mean, it's one thing to meet in the treehouse when it's ninety degrees outside but this . . ." A single brown leaf drifted past the window.

"She's right, Amy," said Leah Fox, who was squished between the two of them on the sofa. "We don't normally fit four people on this."

"Unless it's freezing out," added Erin Valdez from the other end. She covered her nose and sneezed.

Amy Evans cracked up. Her friends were right. They did look totally ridiculous, the four of them, all bundled up like this under two blankets on the sofa. It was early November, and St. Louis was having its first cold snap of the season.

"Okay, okay," she said. "I can take a hint. This meeting is officially moved to the kitchen."

"Until next spring?" asked Leah, quickly unfolding her long legs.

"At least until we thaw out," said Amy. She brushed her dirty blonde hair off her glasses and hurried inside, where everyone regrouped around the kitchen table. "Now where were we?" she said, tossing a bag of taco chips on the table.

"We were talking about the next issue," said Erin, rubbing her hands together. "What to write about. I say we should do a public opinion poll. What do you like about living in Kirkridge or something like that."

"Boring," said Robin, tearing into the taco chips. "How about a poll on who has the best house?"

The rest of the girls groaned.

Amy poured some milk into a pan and then dumped half a jar of chocolate syrup on top. "I like Erin's idea," she said diplomatically. As editor in chief of the *Treehouse Times*, it was her job to decide what should go into the paper. "It doesn't have to be bor-

2

ing. There are probably lots of reasons people like living here."

"I like being able to walk everywhere," said Erin. "The stores are all close. And I like all the big trees. They didn't have trees like this in California."

Erin was Amy's best friend, and her family had moved here a few years ago from L.A. when her father got a job teaching biology at Kirkridge High. Erin was born in L.A., but her parents were both from Mexico. She had short dark hair and dark eyes and was just about the best athlete Amy had ever seen. She wasn't stuck-up about it, either.

Amy set four mugs on the table and nodded thoughtfully. "Cocoa, anyone?" She liked living in Kirkridge, too. Kirkridge was actually a suburb of St. Louis. It had been built in the 1930s and '40s. Amy loved the old-fashioned houses, the sidewalks, and the downtown shopping area. Everyone knew one another in Kirkridge, too, which was one reason the girls' neighborhood newspaper was so popular.

"None for me," said Leah. "Celeste says chocolate is bad for your skin." Celeste was Leah's mother.

"Complete myth," said Robin. "Have the cocoa."

3

Amy nodded. "Actually, what I was thinking," she said, "was that we should devote the next issue to the Thanksgiving food drive."

"Great idea," said Erin, who always agreed with Amy anyway.

Another nice thing about living in Kirkridge was all of its traditions. Besides the food drive, there was the Memorial Day parade, the mother-daughter dinner in the spring, the fireman's ball in October, and the Fourth of July fireworks and picnic party.

"What would we write about?" asked Robin, handing Leah the cocoa. Robin's family had lived in Kirkridge forever.

"We could list the collection times," said Amy. "We could interview this year's chairman."

"I have an idea," said Leah. "Maybe we could volunteer the treehouse as a collection center, since it's getting too cold to be up there anyway."

"Okay!" said Amy. "Does anybody know who the chairman is this year?"

"Aunt Dinah," said Robin.

"*Your* Aunt Dinah?" said Erin. "Matt's mother?" Matt O'Connor happened to be the cutest boy in the entire sixth grade at Kirkridge Middle School. Erin turned to

Amy. "If you want, I'll go interview Mrs. O'Connor."

"Maybe she'd like to come here," said Amy, "to check out the treehouse."

Robin coughed.

"What's wrong?" said Erin.

"I don't think Aunt Dinah could fit through the hatch."

Amy giggled. "You're right. I guess we should go to her house, then."

"Do you still want me to do the poll?" said Erin.

"I don't know," said Amy. "Does anyone else have any news?"

"Mrs. Hunt had her baby," said Robin. "The Delucas are putting on an addition."

"We can put that in our 'What's Happening' column," said Amy, writing down the information. "Anything else?" She turned to Leah, who was their official art director and photographer. "Maybe you can draw something Thanksgiving-y for the front page."

Leah stared off into space and took tiny bites from a taco chip. "Hmmmm."

"How about one of those horns filled with fruit?" said Erin. Leah was the best artist around, but sometimes her ideas were very bizarre, which was why the others tried to

5

give her good suggestions without seem-
ing too obvious about it. Lately, for in-
stance, Leah had started wearing all black.
With her long, dark hair, she looked sort of
like she belonged in a scary Halloween
movie.

"Hmmm," said Leah again.

"That sounds good to me," Robin said,
a little too enthusiastically. Robin had
bright red hair and freckles and a loud,
loud voice.

"I was thinking . . ." said Leah slowly,
still working on the same taco chip.
"Maybe I could draw some of the more familiar people in the neighborhood dressed
as Pilgrims."

For the second time that day, Robin
coughed.

"That might work," said Amy.

Amy's older brother, Patrick, barged into the kitchen. "Hey, bat face," he told
Amy, "who said you could wear my sweatshirt?"

Amy's face turned red.

"Stop bothering us," said Robin. "Can't
you see we're having a meeting?"

Patrick hooted and then grabbed the bag
of taco chips off the table. "Fine by me. I'm
leaving."

"Good riddance," Amy muttered. Ever

6

since Patrick had vacated the treehouse and gotten a motorbike, he'd been completely rude to everyone in the family. Mrs. Evans had told him recently that if he didn't shape up, he was going to have the bike taken away.

"Do you want me to call Aunt Dinah and see if we can go interview her?" asked Robin.

"I'll do it," said Erin.

"That's okay," said Robin. "I know the number by heart." She dialed. "Hello? Matt? It's Robin. Is Aunt Dinah home?"

Erin looked like she was about to have a heart attack.

"Hi, Aunt Dinah," said Robin. "Our newspaper wants to do a big story about the food drive." She paused. "I'm glad you're glad. We wanted to know if we could come over and interview you." Robin listened for another minute and then said, "She wants to know when we can come to her house."

"Anytime," said Amy.

Robin relayed the message. "How about tomorrow at four?" she asked the girls.

"We'll be there," said Erin.

Amy burst out laughing.

"What's so funny?" said Erin.

"You," said Amy.

It was a strange thing about Erin and boys. Ever since Amy had known Erin, she'd never been interested in them . . . until a few weeks ago when Matt O'Connor asked her to help him organize a boys against girls kickball game. Even though the girls lost, ever since then all Erin could think about was Matt, Matt, Matt. Luckily, she didn't talk about him too much.

Erin blushed. "Is the meeting over?"

Amy nodded. "Do you still want to do the opinion poll?"

"If everyone helps me. I'll make up some questions tonight, okay?" Erin was so dependable. It was one of her best features.

They were interrupted by a knock at the door. "Who is it?" yelled Robin.

Amy got up to see. "It's Jamie, Erin." Jamie was Erin's six-year-old brother.

Erin frowned. "What are you doing here?"

Jamie stood in the doorway, nervously gripping the side of his pants. "Danielle is looking for you. She said it's an urgency."

"You mean emergency?" said Amy.

Jamie nodded. Danielle Stevens was a classmate of theirs.

"Where is she?" said Erin.

"On the phone."

"Now?"

Jamie nodded. "It's an urgency."

8

Erin threw up her hands. "Sorry, guys." She got up to leave.

"Wait," said Amy. "Maybe we should come with you and see what's wrong. It could be a story."

"Nah," said Erin. "Nothing exciting ever happens to Danielle."

But Amy had a funny feeling about this. "Just in case," she said, grabbing her jacket. "Robin?"

"If you don't mind, I think I'll stay here," she said, helping herself to more cocoa. "I've been running around all day."

"Me too," said Leah.

Amy didn't have time to argue. She quickly followed Erin out the door and over to her house, which was only a few doors down. Inside, Erin's mother was getting dinner started. Mrs. Valdez worked nights as a private duty nurse. "Danielle said she couldn't wait any longer. She said for you to meet her on the kickball field."

"Now?" said Erin, looking outside. "It's already getting dark."

Mrs. Valdez shrugged her shoulders. "That's what she said." She smiled. "Try not to be too long, okay? Supper's almost ready and I need you to watch Jamie tonight."

Erin wrinkled her nose. "Where's Dad?"

"He has a meeting at school."

Erin sighed. "How come I always get stuck with Jamie? Christopher should have to take a turn, too." Christopher was Erin's older brother.

"Christopher has a basketball game tonight," said her mother. "Otherwise, I'd ask him."

"Come on, Erin," said Amy. "Let's go see what she wants."

The kickball field was on a vacant lot a few blocks from Amy's house. Amy wasn't big on sports, but she knew that the field was very popular.

"Hi, Danielle!" called Erin, as they headed toward the lot. In the distance, they could see her huddled on the field.

Danielle hurried over.

"What's going on?" said Erin.

"You'll never believe it," she said. "Look!"

Right behind home plate was a new sign:

FOR SALE BY OWNER.

Erin's eyes grew wide. "They're going to sell our diamond? But where will we play?"

"How about the school yard?" said Amy.

"Too far," said Erin. She shook her head.

10

"This is awful. Why would the owner want to sell? This lot has been here forever."

Just then a big maroon car pulled up. A fashionably dressed blonde woman with one of those stiff beauty parlor hairdos got out and began walking around. "Mrs. MacKay!" said Amy. "What are you doing here?"

Mrs. MacKay gave Amy a surprised look. "Oh, hello, Amy. I'm here to look at the lot."

"Who's that?" whispered Erin.

"One of the realtors who works with my mom," she whispered back. Amy's mother managed a real estate office downtown.

Amy introduced the girls to Mrs. MacKay.

"How come they're selling this lot?" demanded Erin.

Mrs. MacKay paused. "I don't know. I'm not even sure who's selling it."

Danielle stuck out her lip. "But it's always been for the kids to play on," she said. "It's not fair."

Mrs. MacKay nodded. "I understand how you feel. You must be sorry to see it being sold."

Amy had an idea. She turned to Erin and said, "If you want, I can find out from Mom who owns the lot and you can go talk to him.

11

It would probably make an interesting story."

Erin nodded and stared out at the diamond.

Mrs. MacKay smiled. "If I were you, girls, I wouldn't worry about it too much. A property like this can sit for a long time. It takes just the right buyer."

"Will a house be built on it?" asked Danielle.

"Probably not," said Mrs. MacKay. "This is a commercial lot, which means it's being sold as a business property."

"Another store?" said Erin.

"Another store," said Mrs. MacKay.

Erin scuffed the ground with her toe. Amy could tell she was upset. Erin's biggest passion in life, besides Matt O'Connor, was kickball.

It had grown dark. "Can I give you girls a lift home?" said Mrs. MacKay.

"Sure," said Amy. They all three climbed into the back of Mrs. MacKay's car and she put on some elevator music.

"Who should I drop first?" she said, heading slowly up the block.

"Probably me," said Amy.

Erin still hadn't said anything. Amy was starting to get worried. "Are you okay?" she whispered.

12

"No," said Erin.

"Why not?" said Amy.

Erin swallowed. "Because," she said. "I know who owns the lot."

"You do?" said Amy. "Who?"

Erin looked at her again. "It's Mrs. Allison," she said. "You know. The one everyone calls the Crazy Lady."

Chapter Two

Amy said to Erin, "How do you know the Crazy Lady owns it?"

"She showed up last week when we were playing kickball," said Erin.

"I don't remember that," said Danielle.

"You had a dentist's appointment, remember?"

"Oh, yeah," said Danielle.

"She walked right up to the pitcher's mound in the middle of a game and just stood there, staring at us," said Erin.

"*Weird*," said Amy.

Erin continued. "We didn't know what to do, so we kept playing. Then finally she said, 'You girls are playing to perfection!' "

Amy wrinkled her nose. "She did? Then what?"

Erin shrugged. "Katherine Wolf said, 'Thank you.' "

Amy cracked up. Since most people in Kirkridge were pretty normal, the Crazy Lady's activities were always a big topic. Actually, she wasn't really crazy. Just very, very weird. Even though she was pretty old, she always wore tons of makeup and piled her dyed blonde hair on top of her head like a beauty queen. But that wasn't all. She spoke with a Southern accent and lived by herself in a great big house on Roosevelt Street with her eighteen dogs and six (by last count) cats. Amy's mother had told her that at one time the Crazy Lady had been very rich, but now she just pretended to be.

Mrs. MacKay's voice floated over the back seat. "Amy, dear, you're home."

Amy said to Erin, "Call me in five minutes, okay?"

Erin nodded.

Amy slid across the leather seat. "Thanks, Mrs. MacKay."

"Anytime," said Mrs. MacKay with a polite wave. "My best to your family."

Inside the Evanses kitchen, Amy's father was busy making a salad. David Evans was famous for his salads and his barbeque

15

sauce. "Where've you been?" he asked, tossing a handful of herbs on top of the romaine.

"With Erin," she answered. "Excuse me, Dad." She hurried downstairs to the phone in the family room. "Go on," she said, after Erin had picked up the phone on the other end.

"So there we were on the pitcher's mound," said Erin. "The Crazy Lady kept staring and staring. We started losing our concentration. Finally she said, 'Did you know this is my lot?' We were shocked. Katherine said, 'Is it okay for us to play here?' 'Oh, absolutely,' she said. 'I'm certainly not using it right now.' Then she left."

"Weird," said Amy a second time. "Do you think she's telling the truth?"

"I don't know," said Erin. "You said you could find out, right?"

"Right," said Amy. "I'll ask Mom tonight at dinner."

At the bus stop the next morning, Erin looked the best Amy had ever seen her. Erin wasn't a slob or anything, but she usually just wore jeans and a sweatshirt. Today she had on a really nice jean skirt and navy tights.

16

"Did you talk to your mom?" asked Erin, checking her new sweater for lint.

"She said she'd look it up," said Amy.

"It's official," said Robin, bursting onto the scene. "The Gannons are getting a divorce!"

Amy gasped. "Robin! That's horrible! How do you know?"

"Trish Gannon told my sister Hilary last night. They're selling their house and moving to Ohio."

Leave it to Robin to always be the first with gossip. Amy checked her watch. The bus should have been here by now. On the other side of the street, a few of the boys were playing touch football.

"What do you think happened to John?" said Erin. "Do you think the bus broke down again?"

From across the street Roddy Casper yelled, "If you're so worried about it, why don't you call a taxi?"

"Nobody asked you, Roddy," Robin shouted back. "Do you want to be late for school?"

"*Yes,*" said Roddy and his friend, Grant Taylor. Roddy lived next door to Amy with his ancient grandmother. No one had ever seen his parents, although Roddy always bragged that his father was a helicopter pilot. Roddy had crooked teeth and brown hair that stuck out all over the place because he had cowlicks. He was sort of short and skinny, and he tried to make up for it by acting tough. His best friend, Grant, for example, was twice his size.

Amy, Erin, and Robin sat down on the curb to wait and played a few games of Charades. Chelsea Dale finished her homework from the night before. "Where *is* he?" said Amy. "It's been almost a half hour."

Just then Chelsea's mother drove past in her van. "What are you kids still doing here?" she said.

"The bus never came," said Erin.

Mrs. Dale threw open her doors. "Not again! We went through this last week. Get in. I'll take you."

Everyone except Roddy and Grant got in.

"Aren't you coming?" said Mrs. Dale.

"We're going to wait for the bus," said Roddy.

Mrs. Dale shook her head. "Are you sure, boys?"

"Positive," said Grant.

Mrs. Dale said, "Promise me one thing, then. If it doesn't show up in fifteen minutes, please call the school and let them know you're here, okay?"

"Okay," said Roddy, grinning. The two boys waved wildly as the van drove off.

Amy didn't think much about Grant and Roddy for the rest of the day. Not, that is, until English, the last period, when she noticed Roddy still hadn't shown up. "What do you think happened to them?" she asked Erin, who was her seat partner.

Erin stabbed at a large rubber eraser with her ballpoint pen. "I don't know. Maybe they're still waiting at the bus stop."

Amy began to giggle. The thought of Roddy and Grant standing there all day was too much.

"Ms. Evans," said Mr. Parkinson, the teacher. "*What* is so funny?"

Just then the principal, Mr. Bottomly, walked in. And right behind him was Roddy Casper.

"Mr. Parkinson," said Mr. Bottomly, "excuse me for interrupting but I have a wayward student to return to you."

Roddy gave a sheepish grin.

"It seems that Mr. Casper and Mr. Taylor have been waiting since 8:30 this morning for the school bus."

The class burst out laughing.

"I've told Roddy and Grant that they're to stay for detention study hall for the rest of the week to make up for their unfortunate lack of judgment today."

Roddy stopped smiling.

Mr. Bottomly went on. "I hope, students, that in the event that the bus doesn't make it, as happened this morning, that you will phone either a parent or the school to notify them that you need a ride." He turned sternly to Roddy. "You may take your seat, Mr. Casper."

At four o'clock sharp, Amy, Erin, and Robin stood waiting outside the O'Connors' house. "Where is Leah?" said Amy, looking anxiously up the block.

Leah was the only one of the four who didn't go to Kirkridge Middle School. Instead, she went to private school.

"There she is," pointed Erin.

Leah hurried up to them. "Sorry, guys," she said. "I forgot my camera so I had to go back for it."

"Are we ready?" said Amy.

Erin and Robin nodded.

"You look sort of pale," Robin said to Erin. "Are you getting sick?"

"No," said Erin. She stared at the O'Connors' front door. "Do you think Matt's home?"

"How should I know?" said Robin. "I'm not his mother."

They all followed Robin up to the door. "Hi, Aunt Dinah," said Robin. She walked into the living room. "You guys can sit anywhere you want except Uncle John's chair. Right, Aunt Dinah?"

Mrs. O'Connor beamed. She had a short mother-type hairdo and rosy cheeks. "I'm so glad your paper is doing this for us," she said. "We love free publicity!"

"No sweat," said Robin. "We do stuff like this all the time."

Erin was peering around the room, looking for signs of Matt. She'd told Amy earlier that she hadn't seen him all day at school.

"Well, I'm really enjoying your newspaper," Mrs. O'Connor was saying. "So informative."

Robin gave Amy a little nudge.

"Thank you," said Amy politely. "We like doing it." She settled onto the sofa. "We have some questions to ask you." As usual, they would start with the W-H formula. The W-H formula was something that all newspapers used when they wrote stories. It stood for What, Who, When, Where, Why, and How. A well-written story was supposed to answer each of the five W's and the H.

21

"What exactly is the food drive?" Amy began.

"Well," said Mrs. O'Connor, "as you know, the food drive is a community collection effort which Kirkridge does every Thanksgiving."

"Who gets the food?" said Robin, taking over.

"Needy families in the area," said Mrs. O'Connor. "We get most of their names from the social service agencies." She paused. "Actually, a few of the needy families live right here in Kirkridge."

Amy was surprised. Poor people? In their neighborhood? She knew most people in Kirkridge weren't rich, but had always thought that they had everything they needed.

"Like who?" said Robin.

"That's confidential," said Mrs. O'Connor.

Robin leaned forward. "Can you give us a hint?"

"Robin . . ." said her aunt in a don't-push-it tone of voice.

"Sorry," said Robin.

After the interview was over, as the girls were walking back to Amy's house, they talked again about what Mrs. O'Connor had said. "Did you know there were needy people in our neighborhood?" said Robin.

"I sure didn't," said Erin, shaking her head. Poor Erin. Matt had never shown up and she'd worn all her good clothes for nothing.

"I was thinking," said Robin. "We should try and find out who they are and get a personal interview. You know. Like the real paper does, so that people can contribute money or stuff."

Amy shook her head. "I don't know, Robin. Kirkridge is a small town."

"So what?" said Robin.

"So maybe they don't want people to know."

"Why not?" said Robin. "Isn't the whole point of a newspaper to help people?"

Amy thought it over. "Yes. But people are also entitled to their privacy."

"What do you mean?" said Robin. "We'd be doing them a favor."

Amy shook her head a second time. "I think we should forget it."

Robin scowled. "And I don't."

No one said anything more. Not for now at least. But knowing Robin, the others knew the subject wasn't going to be dropped.

"My mom found out who owns the kickball field," said Amy to Erin a few days later. "You were right. It belongs to Mrs. Allison."

"It does?" said Erin. She shook her head slowly. "Why do you think she's selling it? Do you think she needs the money?"

"Maybe," said Amy. "Do you still want to interview her?"

Erin thought for a moment. "Will you come with me?" she said. "All that staring makes me nervous."

Late that afternoon, Amy's and Erin's feet were crunching along the gravel driveway leading up to Mrs. Allison's house. Unlike most of the houses in Kirkridge, hers was set far back from the street. When they got up close, they could see that the paint was peeling badly and sections of the porch stairs were rotting out.

Amy picked her way across the porch and then pushed the bell. A chorus of dogs began barking. "Maybe we should have called first," Amy shouted over the barks.

"Too late now," Erin yelled back.

Mrs. Allison, dressed in a long purple robe covered with dog and cat hair, threw open the door. "My land!" she exclaimed. "Children!" She pushed the dogs back inside and stepped out on the porch. "What brings you here, precious creations?" She gave a huge smile.

"Uh, we're from the *Treehouse Times*,"

said Amy, pulling an old copy out of her backpack.

"Lovely," said Mrs. Allison. "I'll take one." Inside, the dogs were still barking.

"No, no," shouted Erin. "We always leave one in your mailbox. Haven't you ever seen it?"

"I don't believe so," said Mrs. Allison. Amy noticed that her lipstick was on crooked.

"We'd like to interview you for the paper," said Amy. "There's something we'd like to discuss with you."

"With me?" said Mrs. Allison. "Why, I'm flattered!" She turned around and yelled through the door, "HUSH, NOW." The dogs stopped.

Mrs. Allison brushed her hair back. "Oh, dear," she said. "And I look so terrible, too. Like something the cat dragged in. I never find the time to go to the beauty parlor anymore." She gave her big smile again. "Would you care to come in?"

Amy giggled. "Okay."

Mrs. Allison stepped around a few of the dogs. "I'm sorry the place is so disheveled. One of my dogs, Lancelot, has been sick for weeks now and of course all of my time is taken up with him."

Erin whispered into Amy's ear. "What's disheveled?"

"Messy," said Amy.

Mrs. Allison led them to a chintz sofa strewn with old newspapers and blankets. A couple of the dogs jumped up. "Down," said Mrs. Allison. She cleared a space for Amy and Erin. "Can I get you girls a drink?"

"We're too young," said Erin.

"Heavens, no," said Mrs. Allison. "I didn't mean *that* kind of a drink. I meant a soda pop."

"Oh," said Amy. Out of the corner of her eye, she could see the kitchen. Dishes were piled everywhere. Opened boxes of crackers and pet food littered the counter. On the edge of the sink, an old gray cat lay sleeping. "I think I'll pass," she said.

"Me too," said Erin. She got out her notebook. Mrs. Allison was staring again. "Uh, we heard that you want to sell the kickball lot," she began.

"Kickball lot?" said Mrs. Allison.

"The lot on the intersection of Pierce and Tyler," said Amy.

"That old thing?" said Mrs. Allison. "That belonged to my late husband, Harold. I'd completely forgotten about it until my accountant, Edward Gaines, phoned the other day to remind me. I think it had some taxes due." Several of Mrs. Allison's dogs had joined them on the couch. She scratched a

26

fat little white poodle behind the ears. "My vet bills are astronomical, aren't they, Duchess?"

Duchess bared a few yellow teeth.

"Is that why you want to sell the lot?" asked Amy. "To pay your vet bills?"

Mrs. Allison gave an embarrassed little laugh and leaned over Erin's shoulder. "What are you writing, precious?"

"I'm taking notes," said Erin.

"I certainly hope you won't print *that*." She sniffed.

"Why are you selling the lot, then?" said Amy.

Mrs. Allison fluffed up her robe, causing millions of little animal hairs to fly around the room. "Well," she said. "Well, I suppose because I don't need it."

"It's been our kickball diamond forever," said Erin. "It's the only place around where we can play."

Mrs. Allison smiled. "Really?"

Erin nodded.

"And do you play?" Mrs. Allison continued.

"It's my favorite sport," said Erin. "I'm a pitcher."

"That's fun," said Mrs. Allison. "I played tennis when I was a girl. I was quite a player." She turned politely to Amy. "How about you? Do you participate in a sport?"

"Not really," said Amy. She changed the subject. "When did Mr. Allison buy the lot?"

Mrs. Allison fanned herself with the back of her hand. "Darling, I never followed Harold's business transactions. Can I offer you a cracker?"

"No, thanks," said Amy. Mrs. Allison sure was weird.

Erin signaled to Amy. "Well, thanks, Mrs. Allison," she said, standing up.

Mrs. Allison seemed surprised. "Leaving so soon?"

"I have a piano lesson," said Amy, thinking fast.

"How lovely!" said Mrs. Allison. "With whom do you study?"

"Uh, Mrs. Karnovsky," said Amy.

"Wonderful," murmured Mrs. Allison. She was staring again.

Amy practically tripped over a dog while she was trying to get out of there. Mrs. Allison was definitely giving her the creeps.

"Piano lessons?" said Erin, after Mrs. Allison had told them "bye bye and thank you for coming" about twelve times.

"I had to think of something," said Amy, hurrying onto the street.

"Now what?" said Erin.

"I think she's selling the lot because she needs the money," said Amy. "She just didn't want to admit it."

"No way," said Erin. "She's rich. You heard her talk about her accountant. She's only selling because she wants to."

"Well, we don't know that," said Amy. "Do you have enough notes to write a story?"

"I guess," said Erin. "It's not going to be much of a story, though. Too bad she won't change her mind."

"Yeah," said Amy, looking back at the big house. "It is too bad."

Chapter Three

"Question number one," said Erin as she dangled her legs through the hatch in the treehouse floor. "What do you like most about living in Kirkridge?"

"Let me guess," said Robin, who was perched on top of a case of canned pumpkin. "The people."

"Right!" said Erin. "Seventeen people said the people, eleven said the location, five said the shopping—"

"The *shopping?*" interrupted Robin. "What kind of an answer is that? The really good stores are all at the mall."

"Let her finish, Robin," said Amy.

"Forget it," said Erin. "Question number two. What do you like least?"

"The garbage collection," said Leah.

"I would have said the school," said Robin.

"It so happens," said Erin, "that there was no one who thought that. Except you."

"Don't you have any interesting questions?" asked Robin.

"Like what?" said Erin.

"Like . . . if you were stranded on a desert island and you only had three things to eat, what would they be?"

"What does that have to do with Kirkridge?" asked Erin.

"Nothing," said Robin.

From the corner, Leah said, "Avocados stuffed with crabmeat, papayas, and oysters Rockefeller."

Erin threw down her poll. "Maybe we should talk about something else."

"You don't need to be so sensitive," said Robin.

"What about your other story?" asked Amy quickly. "The one about the kickball diamond?"

Erin shook her head. "The weirdest thing has happened," she said. "After we went to talk to Mrs. Allison, the very next day, the field was mowed."

"So?" said Robin.

"So no one has ever mowed it before," said Erin.

"But it's for sale now," said Amy. "Mrs. Allison probably just wants it to look good."

Erin got this smug look on her face. "Oh yeah?" she said. "Then tell me this. Why did she put a bench out there for us?"

"A bench?" said Leah.

"To sit on while we're waiting for our turn to kick."

"Oh," said Leah. "Maybe she felt a little sorry for you."

"I think she felt a little guilty," said Erin. "Still, it's weird, don't you think?"

"I guess so," said Amy. "You never know with Mrs. Allison, though."

"I've decided to have a boy-girl party for my birthday this year," Robin announced a few days later. She picked up another paper bag full of canned goods and carried it over to Leah, who carried it to Erin standing on the treehouse ladder, who passed it to Amy standing inside.

"You're kidding!" said Amy, dumping the contents on the treehouse floor and clearing space for the next bag. "Why?"

"It's more fun," said Robin. "Who cares about going out to lunch with a bunch of girls?"

"You don't *have* to go out to lunch," said Leah. Her birthday was on Halloween, so she always had a great party. This year she and her mother decorated their whole house to look like a haunted castle. It was unbelievable.

"Which boys are you going to invite?" said Erin.

"The cute ones," said Robin. She struggled over to Leah with two grocery bags of Florida oranges. "We've got enough food here to feed the whole neighborhood. When's Aunt Dinah supposed to pick this stuff up?"

"Not for two more days," said Amy. She looked around the treehouse, which was nearly full. Ever since the real paper had listed them as a collection center, they'd been swamped.

"Have you found out anything about the needy families yet?" Amy asked Robin.

"Not yet," said Robin. "I tried to worm it out of Matt, but he's a total loss. He didn't even know Aunt Dinah was the chairman."

"Not much in the brains department," said Leah.

"What did you say?" said Erin.

"Never mind," said Leah.

Erin straightened up and looked around the treehouse. "Are we done now? I thought I'd go over to the diamond and see if anyone wants to play."

"I guess," said Amy.

Erin looked at them all a second time. "Why don't you guys come with me?"

"You're kidding, right?" said Robin.

"Why should I be kidding?" said Erin.

"I got my exercise carrying cans," said Robin.

"Aw, come on," Erin persisted. "You don't have anything better to do right now, do you?"

"But you're ten times better than us," said Leah. "Besides, I have on my good boots."

"Tell you what," said Erin. "Me against you three. Is that fair?"

"I guess," said Amy, who still wasn't sure why Erin was talking them into this. Maybe she thought they needed the exercise. Or maybe she wanted to be sure she had somebody to play with.

They headed up the street.

"You guuuys."

"It's Chelsea," said Leah quickly. "Don't tell her where we're going."

Chelsea stormed up. She was a year younger than the others, and she was always pestering them to let her help with the paper. She also worshipped Leah and was always copying her, which drove Leah crazy.

"Where are you going?" Chelsea asked, right on cue.

"None of your beeswax," said Robin.

This didn't bother Chelsea, which is how she got her pest reputation. "Can I come?"

"NO," said Leah.

"But I have something important to tell Robin."

Robin's face started to turn red. "Tell me later," she said.

"But you asked me to help you find out who the needy families were and I have some information," said Chelsea.

Now Robin's face turned the color of a tomato.

"Robin!" said Amy.

"Her mom is on the committee," Robin said weakly.

"Don't you want to hear what I found out?" said Chelsea. "Mom is going to be delivering some food bags this afternoon."

Robin cleared her throat. "That's nice."

"I was thinking," Chelsea pressed on, "that if you want, you can hide in our van. There's room under the seats."

Robin's eyes darted from Amy to Chelsea. "Why would I want to do that?"

"To see who's getting the food," said Chelsea. "If we fixed the bags so they were on the other side of the van, Mom would never notice you there . . . especially if I threw a blanket over you."

Erin folded her arms. "I think it's a great idea, Robin."

"You do?" said Robin.

"You do?" said Amy.

"Sure!" said Erin. She gave a wicked smile. "You wanted to find out, didn't you? Now's your chance. I hope you're not the type who gets carsick."

Robin turned pale.

"What's wrong?" said Erin.

"What if I get claustrophobia or something?"

"Erin . . ." said Amy.

"I told Mom I'd help her load the car in ten minutes," interrupted Chelsea. "You can pretend to help me and then I can sneak you in at the last minute."

Robin gave them all a helpless look. "I was just going to play kickball," she said feebly.

"That's okay," said Erin in a cheerful voice. "Two against one is probably fairer anyway. Besides, you'll get good exercise loading up the food."

Robin groaned, and with a grim nod, turned to follow Chelsea up the block.

Amy, Erin, and Leah stood there for a minute. "I think you could have been a little nicer, Erin," said Amy finally. "Even if she *was* being nosey."

Erin shrugged. "If she wants to know that

bad, then she should do her own dirty work."

"Still . . ." said Amy. She glanced up the block.

"Don't worry," said Erin. "I don't think Chelsea's plan is going to work."

"Me neither," said Leah. "How can you expect to see anything if you're stuffed under a blanket?"

"Maybe you're right," said Amy.

"I know I am," said Erin. "Come on. Let's go."

As the girls got closer to the vacant lot they noticed a lot of kids playing on the diamond. "Wow," said Erin. "I've never seen this many people out here."

"I guess you don't need us then," said Amy.

Danielle waved to them from the pitcher's mound. "Look!" she pointed.

"What's she pointing at?" said Leah.

Erin gasped. "Oh, my gosh. I don't believe it."

"*What?*" said Amy.

"Bases!" said Erin. "Somebody put real bases down!" She ran over to the diamond. On every base, sturdy plastic mats had been nailed into the ground. "Where did these come from?" she asked Danielle.

"Nobody knows," she said. "Same place as the bench, I guess."

"Mrs. Allison," said Erin softly.

Amy stared at the diamond. It *was* looking better. Why would Mrs. Allison want to do all this, though, if she planned to sell it? Maybe she had changed her mind after all. But if she had, why was the For Sale sign still up?

"Hey, Ryan," said Roddy to Robin the next morning at the bus stop. "What happened to your neck?"

Robin gave Roddy a dirty look. "It's a crick," she said.

Roddy held his stomach and laughed. "You look like an old lady," he howled.

Robin hobbled over to where Erin and Amy were standing. "*You* try spending two hours smashed under a seat and see how *you* feel," she grumbled.

"Did you have any luck?" said Amy.

"Bad luck," said Robin. "My good sweatshirt got caught on one of those springs under the upholstery and I was stuck there until we got back and Chelsea could let me out. I never saw a thing."

"Oh," said Amy, feeling relieved. "I'm sorry."

Robin carefully massaged her neck. "Just

remind me," she said to Erin, "never to listen to *you* again."

It was Saturday morning, and Thanksgiving was just a week and a half away. The treehouse was so full of canned goods that there was only room for one person at a time up there. Inside the Evanses' kitchen, Amy sat trying to finish the story about the food drive to show Mrs. O'Connor before she came to pick up the food in a few minutes.

"How does this sound?" she said to Erin, who had spent the night. "For thirty years, the Kirkridge Thanksgiving food drive has been helping needy families in St. Louis. The food drive collects canned goods and donations from our neighbors and distributes them to poor people."

Erin interrupted. "I thought we changed that to 'people in need.' "

"You're right," said Amy, erasing the offending phrase. She continued. "This year's chairman is Mrs. Dinah O'Connor."

"Matt's mother," added Erin.

Amy made a face and put down her pencil. "Erin, what's so great about Matt O'Connor? He hasn't talked to you since the kickball game."

Erin got this dreamy look on her face. "What's great about him," she said, "is his curly hair, his perfect teeth, and the way he walks down the hall between second and third periods."

Amy gave her a funny look.

"That's the only time I see him," Erin explained.

"Yuck," said Amy.

Outside, a horn honked. "She's here," said Erin. She ran to the kitchen door, opened it, and then slammed it shut again. *"Eeeeee,"* she screamed.

"What's wrong?" said Amy.

"Matt's here. What's he doing here?"

Amy hopped out of her chair. "I don't know. Calm down."

"I can't," said Erin. "I can't even breathe. I think I'm going to hyperventilate."

The front doorbell rang. *"Eeeee,"* said Erin again.

Amy went to answer the door. "Hello, Mrs. O'Connor," she said.

"Hello, dear," said Mrs. O'Connor. "You know Matt, right?"

"Right," said Amy. She looked around for Erin, who had disappeared. She was probably passed out on the kitchen floor. "Let me get my coat," she said.

She hurried back into the kitchen. "Erin, where are you?" she whispered.

A muffled voice came from the broom closet. "In here."

Amy peered inside. Erin was smashed in next to the mop bucket. "Erin, pleeease. We need you to help us with the cans."

"I don't feel too good," said Erin.

Amy pulled open the door. "Would you come on?" she said impatiently. If this was what liking boys did to you, then she didn't want any part of it.

"Okay, okay," said Erin. She reluctantly put on her jacket and followed Amy outside.

At the treehouse, Mrs. O'Connor, Matt, Leah, and Robin were already busy passing bags along. Erin got into the line without so much as looking at Matt.

"Hey, Aunt Dinah," said Robin, "put on your car radio so we can have some music."

"Good idea," she said with a laugh.

With everyone helping, it took no time at all to get the bags down. Next, Mrs. O'Connor divided the food into groups, so that no one would end up with all canned pumpkin or all string beans. After that, everything had to be rebagged and loaded it into her car, where she already had some frozen turkeys waiting.

"Thanks ever so much, girls," said Mrs. O'Connor when they were finally finished. "You were a great help."

41

"You're welcome," said Amy. Erin still hadn't said a single word. Neither had Matt, for that matter. Being the only boy gave him a good excuse, though.

Amy ran inside and got the story about the food drive. "Before you go," she said, "would you like to read our story?"

Mrs. O'Connor looked it over. "That's lovely," she said. "How soon does your paper come out?"

"The Monday before Thanksgiving," said Amy.

"Wonderful," said Mrs. O'Connor with a nod. She got into her car, where Matt had been sitting for the past ten minutes. "See you later, girls."

"Bye," said Robin and Leah. Erin sighed.

"What is with you?" said Robin.

"Nothing," said Erin, still in a daze.

Amy said, "Maybe we should go check the treehouse and make sure it's all empty."

"I'll go," said Robin. "I think I left my gloves in the crow's nest." She hurried off.

Leah turned to Erin. "Are you okay?"

"Uh huh," said Erin.

Amy rolled her eyes at Leah.

They were suddenly interrupted by Robin, who had stuck her head out of the window of the treehouse and was wildly waving her arms. "You guys! Come quick!"

She disappeared back inside. "What is it?" said Amy, rushing over to the ladder.

"Up here," she shouted. "In the crow's nest."

Amy climbed through the hatch that led into the main room and then up the ladder and through the next hatch to the crow's nest, where she saw Robin, dangling out over a branch. "What is it?" Amy said.

Below them in the main room, Erin called up, "What's wrong?"

Robin pointed through the branches. "Do you see what I see?" she said.

Amy noticed a station wagon parked next door in the Casper's driveway. "Is that your Aunt Dinah's car?" she said.

"It sure is," said Robin. "And look what she's doing."

Amy stared closer. "Oh, my gosh," she said. "She's getting out some bags of groceries and a frozen turkey and . . ." Her eyes followed Mrs. O'Connor from her car to the Casper's front door. "And now she's giving the food to Mrs. Casper!"

From below, Leah said, "What's going on, guys? Tell us what's happening."

Amy opened the hatch to the main room and leaned down. "Robin just discovered one of the needy families in our neighborhood."

43

"Well, who is it?" said Erin.

As Amy hesitated, Robin suddenly leaned down over her right shoulder. "I'll tell you who it is," she cut in. "It's Roddy. Roddy Casper and his grandmother!"

Chapter Four

"I never knew Roddy was poor," said Erin.

"Me neither," said Robin. "He always has nice clothes."

"Just because you're poor doesn't mean you go around looking bad," said Amy.

"But he just got a real boa constrictor for his last birthday," said Erin. "They cost a fortune."

"So?" said Amy. "Maybe his grandmother saved up for it for a long time since she knew Roddy really wanted it."

"Ugh," said Leah. "Why would anyone want anything that disgusting?"

"It doesn't surprise me with Roddy," Robin commented.

"Does Mrs. Casper have a job?" asked Erin.

"I don't think so," said Amy. "She's pretty old. She probably lives on her savings." She sighed. "I never thought of Roddy like this before, did you guys?"

"No," said Erin. "I only think of him as a creep."

Leah stared out at the street. "It must be hard for Roddy's grandmother to have an extra person to feed."

Robin nodded her head in agreement. "Roddy eats a lot for a skinny person, too."

"What can we do to help?" said Leah.

Amy thought for a minute. "I don't know," she said. "Maybe we can ask them if there's something they need."

"I still say we should do a story," said Robin.

"I don't know . . ." said Amy.

"If you're not sure, why don't you just ask them?" said Leah. "They can always say no."

"Maybe you're right," said Amy slowly.

Robin slid down through the hatch. "Who wants to come with me?"

"I can't," said Erin. "I've got a kickball game."

"And I've got an art class at the museum," said Leah.

"I'll go," said Amy. "Just let me get my notebook."

A few minutes later, Amy and Robin knocked on the Caspers' front door.

As they were waiting, Robin said, "Let me do the talking for a change, okay?"

"Okay," said Amy. She hesitated a second and then added, "Just don't be obnoxious."

"Since when am I obnoxious?" said Robin.

Just then Mrs. Casper opened the door.

"Hi," said Robin. "We were thinking about doing a story about poor people in Kirkridge and we were wondering if you were interested."

Mrs. Casper's eyes opened wide.

Amy gave Robin a good poke. "Ow," said Robin.

"Hello, Mrs. Casper," said Amy in her nicest voice. "How are you today?"

"I'm okay," said Mrs. Casper. "How 'bout yourself? You here to see Rod?"

"No," said Amy. "We—"

"Actually," Robin cut in, "we're here to see you."

"What Robin is saying" said Amy, through her teeth, "is that our paper is doing its next issue on the Thanksgiving food drive."

"Is that right?" said Mrs. Casper.

47

"And we noticed that my Aunt Dinah just dropped off some food for you," Robin piped in.

Amy leaned over. "Slow down, would you?" she whispered into Robin's ear.

"It's *my* story," Robin whispered back.

Mrs. Casper's mouth formed a tight line. "What are you getting at?" she said.

Amy interrupted again. "We thought it might be nice to do a story about a needy family in Kirkridge for our Thanksgiving issue," she explained.

Mrs. Casper's eyes suddenly narrowed. "A story about us?"

"To let people know that you need help," said Robin.

"We don't need help," snapped Mrs. Casper. "And where do you get off, butting into other people's business?"

"But—" said Robin.

"Darn kids," said Mrs. Casper. She slammed the door shut.

Amy and Robin just stood there. "That was weird," said Robin finally. "You'd think she'd be grateful."

Amy turned to Robin, slightly peeved. "I told you we shouldn't have interfered."

"What do you mean?" said Robin.

Amy threw up her arms in exasperation.

48

"People are entitled to their privacy. I told you it was none of our business."

Robin stared forlornly at the house. "No one's ever slammed a door on me before."

Amy took Robin's arm and tried to pull her away. "Come on. Let's get out of here."

But instead of following Amy, Robin walked back up to Mrs. Casper's door and knocked again.

"What are you doing?" said Amy.

"Maybe we didn't explain ourselves right," said Robin.

Mrs. Casper opened the door. "Now what?" she said.

"Uh, you know how the real paper does stories around the holidays on people who need help? Like there was one I read about a little boy who wanted his own bicycle."

"Rod has a bicycle," said Mrs. Casper tersely.

"But maybe there's something else he needs," Robin persisted. "Or you need. We can write it up in the paper and then—"

"I thought I told you to mind your own business," said Mrs. Casper. "I don't need the whole neighborhood knowing about my troubles." She shut her door again.

"See?" said Amy under her breath. "I *told*

49

you they didn't want it blabbed all over the neighborhood."

Robin turned to her. "But the real paper does stories on needy families all the time."

"But they use initials," Amy responded. "Not people's real names."

"So? We could use initials," said Robin. "We could even make up names."

Amy sighed. "Everyone would still know who we were talking about," she said. "Kirkridge isn't that big."

Robin made a face. "I never get to do my ideas," she grumbled.

"That's not true," said Amy.

"It is true," said Robin. She turned toward her house. "All I was trying to do was help," she called over her shoulder. "What's wrong with that?"

Amy spent the rest of the afternoon curled up on the living room sofa reading her new science fiction trilogy. She loved books that made her imagination wander. She had just gotten to the part where Josie, the heroine, was attempting to outwit the evil Zorka through mental telepathy when Patrick rudely interrupted her.

"Phone call," he blasted into her ear.

She looked up with a start. "For me?"

"No, the sofa," said Patrick in a sarcastic voice.

Amy gave him a dirty look.

"Don't talk too long," said Patrick. "I'm expecting a call from someone." Someone usually meant a girl.

Amy hurried into the kitchen. "Hello?" she said, picking up the phone.

"It's me," said Erin on the other end. "How did it go with Mrs. Casper?"

"Not great," said Amy. She explained what had happened.

"So you were right," said Erin. "We shouldn't write a story."

"Try telling that to Robin," Amy sighed. "By the way, how was your kickball game?"

"That's why I'm calling," said Erin. "Guess what Mrs. Allison added now? A backstop!"

"You're kidding," said Amy. "A real one?"

"Yep," said Erin. "It's nice, too. It must have been installed yesterday, while we were in school."

Amy said, "It must feel like Christmas to you."

"It does," said Erin. "And now that we've got a real diamond, a lot more kids are playing. I don't know why she's doing this, but it sure is great."

"I don't either," said Amy slowly.

51

"Anyway," said Erin. "I'm not going to worry about it. I just wanted to tell you what was up."

Patrick barged into the kitchen and stood next to the phone, looking impatient.

"Uh, I've got to go," said Amy. "I'll talk to you tomorrow, though, okay?"

"Okay," said Erin. "What are you doing tomorrow?"

"I have Sunday school in the morning," said Amy. "Then nothing."

"If my mom says it's okay, do you want to go to Aegean Pizza with us for lunch?" The Valdezes went out for pizza every Sunday after Mass. It was a family tradition.

"Sure," said Amy. Patrick had started to drum on the wall with two chopsticks.

"What's that noise?" said Erin.

"A pest," said Amy. "A five-foot eight-inch pest." Patrick tapped on her glasses with the chopsticks. "Ow. I've gotta go, okay?"

"Okay," said Erin. "I'll call you later when my mom gets home from work."

At the big back table in Aegean Pizza, Amy sat surrounded by the Valdez family. They all had on their jeans, which made Amy wish she were a Catholic. The Catholic kids could

52

wear jeans to Mass instead of getting dressed up.

When Mr. Petropoulus, the owner, came over and saw Amy sitting with the Valdezes he said, "Ah, Mrs. Valdez, I see you have a black ship in your family today."

"A black ship?" said Mrs. Valdez.

Mr. Petropoulus pointed to Amy.

"Oh," said Mrs. Valdez. "You mean a black *sheep!*"

"Yes," he beamed. "A black ship. Very nice girl, though."

Erin and Amy laughed. Mr. Petropoulus was a special friend of theirs. He had nicknamed Amy "Ms. Pulitzer" when their paper had first come out.

"What'll it be today?" said Mr. Petropoulus.

"One large gourmet, one large pepperoni, and a small anchovy," said Erin, whose turn it was to order.

Mr. Petropoulus wrinkled his nose. "Who's having anchovies?"

"Dad and Erin," said Jamie, pointing an accusing finger. "Nobody's going to want to kiss them. Hee, hee."

A noisy commotion interrupted the table. "Look!" Erin whispered.

Outside, Mrs. Allison was attempting to tie four of her dogs to a parking meter.

53

Her high spike heels weren't helping matters.

"Michael," said Mr. Petropoulus to his cook, "do me a favor. Go help Mrs. Allison park her dogs."

"Okay, boss," said Michael.

It took a few minutes, but everything finally settled down. "Thank you so much," Mrs. Allison kept telling Michael. "I don't know what I'd have done without you." She gave him a big spidery-looking hug which made his face turn red. Then she started up the street.

"Where's she going?" said Amy.

"Who knows?" said Mr. Petropoulus.

Erin suddenly slid her chair out from under the table. "Mom, may I be excused for a minute? I want to talk to Mrs. Allison."

Erin's father said something in Spanish to her mother, to which Erin said, "Don't worry, I won't." Even though Erin didn't speak Spanish, she always managed to figure out what her parents were saying. "Come on," Erin whispered in Amy's ear.

On the street, Mrs. Allison was still wobbling along on her high heels, saying hello and nodding to everyone, even total strangers.

"Mrs. Allison," called Erin. She and Amy ran up to her. "Remember us?"

"Why, yes, of course," said Mrs. Allison. She smiled at them as if she were a Miss America or something.

"We wanted to thank you for fixing up the diamond," said Erin.

"Diamond?" said Mrs. Allison.

"On the vacant lot," said Erin.

"Oh, you mean Harold's lot!" said Mrs. Allison. "I haven't been past that place for weeks."

"The backstop is great," Erin continued. "It really makes a difference during a game."

"What backstop is that?" asked Mrs. Allison politely.

"The one you installed on Friday," said Erin.

Mrs. Allison shook her head. "I'm sorry, dear, but I still don't know what you're talking about."

Erin stopped. "You don't?"

"No," she said, staring.

"But somebody fixed the diamond up," said Erin. "It has a bench and real bases and a backstop. It's really fun to play there now."

"My, my!" said Mrs. Allison. "Who do you suppose?"

A suspicious look crossed Erin's face. "Are you *sure* you didn't do it?"

"Cross my heart," chirped Mrs. Allison. "It's a lovely thing to do, though, don't you think? Sort of . . . serendipitous."

"I guess," said Erin, who looked totally confused. "What if somebody buys it, though?" said Erin.

Mrs. Allison waved her hand in the air. "Oh, don't worry about that. When the time comes, I suppose you'll just have to leave. In the meantime, though, you have my blessing. Bye, bye, now." She wobbled off.

Amy scratched her head. If Mrs. Allison didn't put up the backstop, then who did? And why? She turned to Erin. "Something is fishy."

"You're telling me," said Erin. "I still think Mrs. Allison did it, though."

"Why?" said Amy.

"I don't know," said Erin. "Maybe she wants to pretend she's our fairy god-mother."

"But a backstop is expensive," Amy said.

Erin shrugged her off. "She probably keeps millions of dollars tucked away in empty cat food cans under her mattress."

Amy stared up the street.

"Come on," Erin interrupted. "I bet our pizza is ready."

"Okay," said Amy, still distracted. "I'm coming."

There was no more discussion about the diamond during lunch. Afterwards, when it was time to leave, Erin said to Amy, "Do you want to come over this afternoon? Dad and I are building a purple martin house."

"What's a purple martin?" said Amy.

"They're these birds that eat mosquitoes," Erin explained. "They only live in one special type of birdhouse." Erin and her father were always doing projects together.

"I think I'll pass today," said Amy politely.

"Are you sure?" said Erin.

"Positive," said Amy. "I actually have something else to do."

"What?" said Erin.

"Nothing important," said Amy, trying her best to brush it off. "Thanks again for the lunch, though."

A few minutes later, Amy was standing in front of Vicky Lamb's house, ringing the doorbell. Vicky was a reporter for the real newspaper, the *St. Louis Post-Dispatch*. She was also the official advisor for the *Tree-house Times.*

"Hi there," Vicky said, when she opened the door and saw Amy. "What brings you here?" She had on her sweats and a head-band.

"Are you busy?" said Amy.

"Just vacuuming," Vicky answered. "Sundays are the only chance I get to clean up. Come on in."

Amy followed Vicky into the living room where they both sat down on big purple floor cushions. Immediately, one of Vicky's three cats (was it Horace or Wendell?) came over and started gently poking its paws up and down and up and down to make a comfortable spot for itself on Amy's lap.

"What's up?" said Vicky. The girls had first met Vicky when she gave their class a tour of the *Post-Dispatch* offices. It was just a coincidence that she lived in Kirkridge.

"I'm not sure yet," Amy answered. She proceeded to tell Vicky all about Mrs. Allison and the mysterious donor. After she finished she said, "It just doesn't make sense."

Vicky nodded thoughtfully. "You're right," she said. "It doesn't. Especially if you're convinced it wasn't Mrs. Allison." She paused. "What do you want to do?"

"I think," said Amy, "I want to do some snooping."

"I was hoping you'd say that," said Vicky with a sly smile. "Sounds like you may have a lead!"

"Do you have any suggestions?" said Amy, reaching into her bag for her reporter's notebook. Amy prided herself on always being prepared.

"First," said Vicky, "I'd try and track down where the equipment came from. You need to go over to the diamond and see if you can find any signs or labels on anything."

"Right," said Amy, scribbling furiously.

"Next," said Vicky, "check the local sporting goods stores. See if they carry the same equipment or if they don't, who does. Try to find out who mowed the field or who installed the equipment."

"Got it," said Amy, still writing. She was so excited her heart was pounding. "What about the listing?" she said. "Should I get my mom to give me the listing?" A listing was a sheet of paper that realtors used to describe a property that was for sale. It told the size, the cost, the location, everything.

"Can't hurt," said Vicky. "Right now you

need to collect as much information as possible. Do you have enough to get started?"

"More than enough," said Amy. She pushed Horace or Wendell off her lap and hopped up. "Thanks a lot."

Vicky grinned. "No problem. Let me know what you find out."

"Don't worry," said Amy. "I will." She hurried off to get started.

Chapter Five

When Amy got home from Vicky's, her father and Patrick were in the living room, watching a football game. Amy's mother was working.

She stuck her head into the room and said, "Dad, I'm going over to the kickball diamond."

"Okay, honey, have fun," her father called back.

Amy let herself out the garage door and hopped onto her bike. She couldn't wait to get started.

Minutes later, she was at the field. She leaned her bike up against the new backstop and tried as inconspicuously as possible to look around.

The vacant lot where the diamond was located was at the intersection of Pierce and Tyler near the center of town. Directly across the street from third base was a gas station, which was handy if you needed to go to the bathroom. On the other corner was an auto parts store, and on the last corner, across from first base, was a small lot with an old decrepit tool shed on it.

"Wanna play, Amy?" said Brendan Myers. A big game was in progress.

"No, thanks," she answered. "I sprained my ankle." For effect, she limped over to the bench and sat down next to a third grader named Paul Hammer.

"How'd you hurt your ankle?" he asked.

"Uh, I tripped on the stairs," said Amy. She quietly pulled her notebook out of her back pocket and got to work. First, the bench. She noted in her notebook that the bench seemed to be very old and worn, but comfortable. It could have been sitting outside somewhere for many years.

"You're up, Paul," shouted Brendan.

As Paul slid off the bench, Amy noticed something else. Carved into the bench were a pair of worn initials. She wasn't sure, but they looked like the letters *T.S.* She wrote them down in her notebook. Next, the bases.

Amy wandered over to first base, remembering to limp. There didn't seem to be any labels on the bases. Not on the tops, at least.

"You're in the way," shouted Brendan.

"Sorry," said Amy. She quickly sketched a picture of the base and wrote a description beside it. She examined the backstop next. It looked like a normal backstop to her, about ten feet tall and made of strong wire fencing. On one of the poles was a small label which said "Jim's Sporting Goods."

As she was writing this information down, Brendan said, "Evans, *what* are you doing?"

"Nothing," she said. She'd never heard of Jim's Sporting Goods, but she could look it up in the phone book when she got home. She went over and sat down on the bench again.

"What happened to your foot?" said a girl named Nicole.

"I tripped," said Amy. She leaned way over and looked underneath the bench. Nothing under there except wads of chewing gum. Then something caught her eye. Across the street, a man in work clothes opened the tool shed door. And inside the shed was a large tractor mower. She sat back up with a jolt.

"Do you know that man?" she asked Nicole.

Nicole looked at her like she was crazy.

"Never mind," she said. She tucked her notebook into her jeans pocket and hurried across the street.

"Excuse me," she said to the man locking up the tool shed. "Is that your tractor?"

"Not exactly," he answered. He pointed to the gas station. "Belongs to Duke. I just help him out."

"I was wondering," said Amy. "Does he ever use it to mow lawns around here?"

The man gave her an amused smile. "He contracts it out to the city," he told her. "Mows in the summer and snow plows in the winter. Why?"

Amy pointed across the street to the vacant lot. "Do you know who mows over there?"

The man grinned. "Nobody, most of the time," he said. "Belongs to the Crazy Lady."

"Somebody mowed it last week, though," Amy persisted.

The man nodded. "I know," he said. "I did."

Amy's heart began to pound. "You did? Did the Crazy Lady hire you?"

"Not this time," said the man. "It was a kid. Sandy hair, medium build. He paid me cash."

Amy took out her notebook and began

scribbling furiously. The man gave her a strange look. "Did you get his name?" she said.

"Nope," he said. "I figured the Crazy Lady sent him."

"Thanks," said Amy. "Thanks very much." She realized it wasn't much to go on, but at least it was a start. She crossed the street and climbed back onto her bike.

" 'Bye, Amy," said Brendan. "Hope your ankle is better."

"Thanks," she called. For a boy, Brendan wasn't bad.

Back at home, Amy's father and brother had finished watching the game. Mr. Evans was paying bills at his desk in the family room and Patrick was in his room, probably listening to music.

Amy brought the phone book over to the kitchen table and looked up Jim's Sporting Goods. "Wedge Avenue, Washington Groves," she said aloud. She dialed their number. "How late are you open today?" she asked.

"Five o'clock," said the salesperson.

Amy glanced at the clock. It was four already.

"Dad," she said, hurrying into the family room. "Can you give me a ride to Washington Groves?"

Amy's father pushed his glasses up on his forehead, the same way Amy always did. "Right now?" he said in an irritated voice.

"Never mind," said Amy. She found Patrick in his room, lying on his bed with his Walkman. "Can you give me a ride to Jim's Sporting Goods?"

Patrick took off his earphones. "In what? Dad's car?" Patrick was only fourteen.

"We could go on your motorbike," said Amy.

"I don't have a permit, remember? I'm not supposed to go on the main streets."

"But this is important," said Amy. "We can take the back roads."

Patrick stared at her suspiciously. "What's so important about Jim's? You taking up football?" He laughed loudly at his own dumb joke.

Amy thought fast. She *had* to make it to Jim's today. She suddenly had an idea. "You know that girl you like?"

"Which one?" said Patrick.

"Jenny Marconi," said Amy. "She's a cheerleader."

"What about her?"

"She lives in Washington Groves, doesn't she? Maybe you can go visit her while I'm at Jim's."

Patrick made a face.

"You have a good excuse," Amy continued. "You can tell her you're waiting for
your sister."

Patrick made another face and then s-l-o-w-
l-y got off his bed. "You're going to have to
wear my football helmet."

"That's okay," said Amy eagerly.

"And don't tell Mom or Dad that I went to
Washington Groves on the bike."

"I won't," said Amy. "I promise. Come on,
let's go."

By the time Patrick dropped Amy off at
Jim's, it was 4:30. Going the back way had
taken a lot longer than she expected, especially since Patrick had insisted on cruising past
Jenny's house first to be sure she was home.

Amy made her way upstairs to the sporting equipment area.

"May I help you?" said a young guy wearing a necktie.

"Do you sell baseball bases?" she asked.
"And backstops?"

He laughed. "Sure. You planning to build
a stadium?"

Amy coughed. "Not really." She pulled out
her notebook and showed him her drawing
of the bases. "Do you sell these?"

"Yep," he said. "How many do you want?"

"Uh, none right now. How often you sell
backstops?"

"Depends," said the salesman. "This time of year, not too many."

"I was wondering," said Amy, choosing her words carefully. "Have you sold any in the past two weeks?"

"As a matter of fact," he said, "I have. I sold one last week that we installed over in Kirkridge at the intersection of Pierce and Tyler." He leaned down. "Why do you want to know?"

"Just curious," said Amy, trying to remain calm. "Do you remember who you sold it to?"

"As a matter of fact," he said, laughing, "I do."

"Who was it?" said Amy quickly.

He shook his head back and forth. "You're pretty curious, aren't you?"

Amy wished the salesman would stop teasing her and just tell her what she wanted. "Somebody put up a backstop on our kickball diamond as a surprise," she said. "We wanted to know who it was."

"Aha!" he said. "I didn't think you wanted to turn your backyard into Busch Stadium."

Amy smiled patiently. This was taking forever. Finally, the guy leaned down again. "I'd like to help you but I can't."

Amy's face fell. "Why not?"

"Because your benefactor paid cash."

"Can you at least tell me what he looked like?" said Amy. "Was he young? Sandy hair? Medium build?"

"She," said the salesman. "It was a she."

"A *she?*" said Amy. Now she was really confused. Maybe Mrs. Allison *was* doing all this. "What did the lady look like?" she asked. "Was she sort of old?"

"Sort of," said the salesman.

"And sort of . . . crazy?"

"A little."

"Dyed blonde hair?"

"No," said the salesman. "Dark brown."

Amy gave a relieved sigh. Then it wasn't Mrs. Allison. At least, it wasn't Mrs. Allison in person. Still, she could have been *sent* by Mrs. Allison. So could the guy with the sandy hair. Amy shook her head. Instead of getting more answers, she was only getting more questions. She said to the salesman, "Do you remember anything else about her?"

"Not really," he answered. "It was very busy in here. Wait. There *was* one thing. She had a very strange purse. It had the head of some sort of dead animal on it."

"A real animal?"

"Yeah," said the man. "You couldn't help noticing it. It had leathery skin and a pointed snout."

Amy shivered. "Okay, thanks," she said.

69

"You've been very helpful." She turned to leave.

"Now tell me the *real* reason you wanted to know who bought that backstop," said the salesman.

Amy shrugged her shoulders. "That *was* the real reason."

The man laughed out loud. "Okay," he said. "If that's what you say." He walked over to another customer. "Excuse me. Do you need some help?"

Amy hurried back downstairs to find Patrick. There were so many unanswered questions. Who was the guy with the sandy hair? And what about the lady with the creepy handbag? How would she ever find them?

"Did you get my invitation?" asked Robin the next morning at the bus stop.

"What invitation?" said Erin.

"To my boy-girl party," she said. "It's next Friday night."

"Not yet," said Erin.

"Me neither," said Amy.

"Well, you will," said Robin. "I invited ten boys and ten girls. No presents, though, or cake. That's for children."

"Is your cousin coming?" said Erin.

"You mean Matt?" said Robin. "Yeah, he's coming."

Amy said, "What are we going to do at your party?"

"Listen to music, eat food, talk."

It sounded like a slumber party, only with boys.

Roddy butt in, "Who's having a party?"

"That's for us to know and you to find out," said Robin. She gave him a funny look. "Hey, where were you on Saturday afternoon when we went to your house?"

Amy's face turned red.

"Whaddya mean?" said Roddy, glancing around at the others.

"Hey, Robin," said Amy, grabbing her by the elbow. "I want to tell you something."

"Ow," said Robin. "Wait."

Amy dragged her over to the bushes. "I think since we aren't going to write the story, we shouldn't say anything to Roddy."

"Why?"

"Because that's his private business."

Robin looked back at Roddy. "But *why?*"

"Robin, *please,*" said Amy.

Robin squinched up her eyes and reached into her pocket for a caramel chewie. "Okay," she said. "I won't say anything."

That afternoon when Amy got home from school, a letter addressed to the editor of the

71

Treehouse Times was waiting for her. Right away, she called Erin.

"We got a letter!" she said.

"Did you read it yet?" said Erin.

"Of course not," said Amy. She always tried to wait for the others when it came to newspaper business.

"Who's it from?" said Erin.

Amy checked the envelope. Whoever it was didn't believe in using capital letters. "There's no return address," she said. "Listen, you call Leah and I'll call Robin, okay? Be here in five minutes."

"See ya," said Erin.

Five minutes later, the four girls were assembled around Amy's kitchen table. "Ready?" she said.

"I hope it's a nice letter this time," said Robin. The only other letter they'd ever received was from Mr. Korn, the owner of the local drugstore, who'd complained about a story they'd written about him.

Amy tore open the envelope. The handwriting on the inside was the same. No capital letters. The letter read:

dear treehouse times,
 for several years now, children have enjoyed playing kickball in the vacant lot on

72

the corner of pierce and tyler. lately, though, this lot has undergone some amazing transformations. what was once an ugly field is now a beautiful baseball diamond, complete with backstop and bases! I think our local businesses should take advantage of this and consider sponsoring some teams. it's high time our merchants got involved with the young people in our community. what do you think? sincerely, an appreciative neighbor.

"Wow! What a great idea!" said Erin. "Why didn't we think of that?"

"None of us plays except you," said Leah.

But Erin wasn't listening. She hopped out of her chair and began circling the table. "We could ask Mr. Petropoulus if he'd sponsor us," she said. "We'll call ourselves the Treehouse Terrors!"

"But none of us plays except you," echoed Robin.

"That doesn't matter," said Erin. "We can get some good players to join us." She lit up. "Hey! Why don't we organize a Thanksgiving charity tournament? The Treehouse Terrors against whoever. We'll put a sign-up sheet up at school."

Leah said, "Maybe instead of selling tickets, admission can be a donation for the food drive."

"Yeah!" said Robin. "Good idea! It'll be great publicity. When should we do it?"

Erin looked at the calendar stuck on the Evanses refrigerator. "I guess next Saturday."

"The day after my party?" said Robin.

"That isn't much time," said Leah.

"Plenty of time," said Erin. "We'll do posters."

Amy still hadn't said anything but now Erin turned to her. "What's wrong?"

Amy shifted uncomfortably. She didn't want to mention anything about her trip to Jim's yet. "What about the fact that the lot is for sale?"

"What about it?" said Erin.

"Well, what if it gets sold?"

"It won't be sold between now and Saturday," said Erin.

"But when the lot does get sold, where will all these new teams play?" said Amy. She was afraid of getting everyone involved and then having them be disappointed.

"Why are you worrying so much?" said Erin. "This is a perfect chance for us to do something for the neighborhood."

"I guess you're right," said Amy. "It's a good way to get everyone involved." She paused. "Do you think Mrs. O'Connor still needs stuff?"

"They collect right up to Thanksgiving," said Robin.

Amy smiled. "Good. Then let's get busy, guys. We've got a lot of work ahead of us."

Chapter Six

"Batter up," said Erin.

Amy ran over to home plate and got ready to kick.

"Now remember what I told you," said Erin. "Keep your eye on the ball. It's easy."

Amy rolled her eyes at Leah and Robin, who were waiting their turns on the bench. This practice was obviously Erin's idea.

Erin pitched the ball. "Now!" she said.

"Ooomph!" Amy swung her leg and missed.

"One more time," said Erin.

This time, Amy kicked the ball past second base. The bench cheered. "Thank you, thank you," said Amy, taking a bow. "Who's next?"

"Me, I guess," said Leah.

Amy sat back down on the bench. She couldn't believe how quickly Erin's idea for a charity tournament had caught on when they'd put up sign-up sheets at school. Here it was Wednesday and they'd already filled three and a half teams. So far, they all had sponsors, too: Aegean Pizza, the Sugar Bowl, and the Copy Corner. And rumor had it the gas station was considering.

Just then Mrs. MacKay's big maroon car pulled up and parked at the curb. A tall, skinny man with curly hair got out on the passenger side and followed her over to the lot.

Amy jumped off the bench. "Hi, Mrs. MacKay," she said.

"Hello!" said Mrs. MacKay. "Fancy meeting you here!" She turned back to the man. "As you can see, you've got a good location here. Busy intersection, good traffic flow." The man carefully studied the lot.

"What about the diamond?" he said abruptly.

Mrs. MacKay smiled. "Er, what about it?"

Erin rushed over from the pitcher's mound. "It's for us kids to play on," she said. "It's the only baseball diamond around. Do you like our new backstop and bases?"

Amy couldn't believe that Erin would interrupt a grown-up's conversation like that, but the man only nodded politely. "Very nice."

Erin kept going. "We just formed a kickball league. Some of the local businesses are sponsoring us."

Mrs. Mackay forced a smile. "But darling, the lot is for sale."

Erin grinned at the man. "You don't *really* want to buy it, do you?" she said. "Say no."

Mrs. MacKay's smile disappeared. "Mr. Werner represents Burger Boy," she said through her teeth. "He's a very important client."

"*The* Burger Boy?" said Robin. "Mmmm. They make the best french fries. Not too greasy, not too crunchy—"

"But, Robin," said Erin, "you can go to the Burger Boy in Washington Groves. There's only one kickball diamond."

"True," said Robin.

"You wouldn't believe how many kids play on this diamond," Erin continued.

The man seemed interested. "How many, would you say?"

"At least fifty," said Erin. She pointed to one of their posters on the fence. "See? We're having a charity tournament on Saturday. The proceeds go to the Thanksgiving

78

food drive. We already have three teams signed up."

Mrs. MacKay took the man firmly by the elbow and steered him past the girls. "Let's have a look around, shall we?"

"Where did you say that other lot was located?" he asked her.

"On the corner of Hayes and Polk," she answered. "It's higher priced than this one, though. And not as good a location."

The girls watched them walk off. "He should buy it," Erin grumbled. "Then we wouldn't have to stop playing."

"But Erin," said Amy. "Somebody is going to buy this lot eventually."

"They *can't,*" said Erin. "Look how many people depend on it. They can't turn it into a Burger Boy."

Poor Erin. Amy felt bad for her. "Come on, Erin," she said. "Let's finish our practice."

Erin scuffed her toe in the dust. "I don't feel like it anymore."

"Are you sure?" said Robin. "We were just starting to improve."

But Erin wasn't about to be cheered up. "Practice is over for today," she said. "I'm not in the mood anymore."

The next afternoon, Amy was sitting in the treehouse with Leah, going over her artwork for the next edition. If the weather was warm enough, Amy always preferred the tree-house to the kitchen. More professional. To-day, though, despite the treehouse, nothing seemed to be going right. Erin was still upset about the diamond and Amy still hadn't found anything else out about the mystery lady.

She studied the little animated fruits and vegetables that Leah had drawn dancing around a cornucopia. "Cute," she said, half-heartedly. She pointed to a plump tomato wearing sneakers. "This one looks sort of like Robin."

Leah giggled. "It is. You're in there, too."

"I am?" said Amy. She stared at the draw-ings with renewed interest. "Is that me?" she pointed. "The banana with glasses?"

Leah nodded. "Top banana. Get it?"

Amy was relieved it wasn't because Leah thought she *looked* like a banana. "What about that pea pod kicking the little pea?" she asked. "Is that Erin?"

"Right," said Leah. "And I'm the string bean with the beret." They both laughed loudly.

"That's really funny," said Amy. "Do you think the others will notice?"

Leah shrugged. "Maybe. I don't really care if they do, though. It's just my own little joke." She looked at the layout for the front page. "What about the story about Mrs. Casper? We decided not to do it, so I don't need to save space, right?"

"Right," said Amy firmly.

Leah stuffed her things into a giant pink and black bag and then said, "I have to go to Korn's to buy some art supplies. Want to come?"

"Sure," said Amy. "Let me get my wallet."

Not long after, Amy and Leah were standing in Korn's, trying out pens on a little pad of test paper. "It has to have just the right feel or it doesn't draw well," Leah was explaining. She drew a purple curly doodle with a smiling face.

"May I help you?" said Mr. Korn.

"We're testing out pens," said Leah.

Mr. Korn grunted. Kids didn't thrill him.

"Excuse me," interrupted a tall woman with dark brown hair. "Where are the mailing envelopes?"

"Next aisle," said Mr. Korn.

Leah bent over to try another pen.

"Are you planning to buy something?" Mr. Korn asked Leah.

"Excuse me," interrupted the woman again. "Where did you say?"

81

"I'll show you," said Mr. Korn.

Leah glanced over and then continued her doodling. She drew a rectangle with a funny-looking animal's head on it. "Did you see that lady's pocketbook?" she said, sketching absentmindedly. "Weird, huh? Look." She pointed to her drawing.

As Amy stared at the picture she suddenly gasped.

"What is it?" said Leah.

Amy bolted around the corner. Mr. Korn was standing by himself, straightening the envelopes. "Do you know where that lady went?" she asked.

"Away," he said.

Amy dashed out into the street. "No!" she cried. "I can't have lost her!"

Leah appeared. "Amy, what's wrong?"

"I have to find that lady," she said, starting up the street.

"Why?" said Leah, hurrying to catch up.

"Because I think she's the one who bought the backstop and the bases for the diamond," said Amy.

"It wasn't the Crazy Lady?" said Leah.

"No," said Amy. "Come on. I'll explain later." She began looking inside every store on the street.

"I'll check the other side," said Leah, crossing over. "What do I do if I find her?"

"Yell," said Amy. At that moment she caught a glimpse of a long black raincoat at the other end of the block. "That's her!" she screamed.

"Where?" said Leah, rushing back.

"She went into Ondine's," said Amy breathlessly. "Let's go."

Amy and Leah charged up the block. Ondine's was a fancy new restaurant which had been open only a few months. They screeched up just as the woman threw open the front doors to leave.

"Pardon me," she said, swooping past them.

This time Amy got a good look at the purse. It was definitely the same purse the man at Jim's had described. No one else in the world could have a purse like that.

"Uh, er, uh, excuse me," said Amy.

When the woman turned around, Amy shivered. She looked just like Cruella De Ville in *101 Dalmations.*

"What is it?" the woman said. She had spikey jet black hair, long red nails, and a thin pointy face.

"Uh, I like your pocketbook," said Amy weakly.

The woman smiled. "Do you?" she said. "It's armadillo. From Texas. One of a kind." She turned to leave.

"Leah, help me," said Amy under her breath. "I have to get her name."

Leah gave Amy a helpless shrug as the woman spun ahead.

Amy panicked. "Follow her!" she said.

Just then a gust of wind came up. As the armadillo lady hurried up the street, the red and purple scarf she had around her neck suddenly blew off. "Wait," called Amy. She grabbed the scarf as it flew past and waved it in the air. "You dropped something."

The armadillo lady kept going.

"No, wait," called Amy. "Don't leave. You dropped your scarf."

The woman climbed into a large white car and drove off.

"Oh, no," Amy wailed. "Now I'll never find her."

Leah rushed up behind her. "Yes, you will," she said. She took the scarf out of Amy's hand. "Follow me. I have an idea."

Leah marched back down the block and straight through the front doors of Ondine's. It took a few minutes for Amy's eyes to get accustomed to the darkness, but once they were, she realized she was standing in some sort of foyer. A man in a suit behind a podium asked, "May I help you?"

Leah boldly said, "One of your customers

just dropped this in front of your restaurant."

"And whom might that be?" he asked.

"It was a tall lady with dark hair," said Leah. "She had an armadillo pocketbook."

The man's face lit up. "Ah!" he said. "You must mean Mrs. Sakbodin. She came in to make a dinner reservation."

"Mrs. Sakbodin?" said Amy.

The man took the scarf. "Why, yes," he said. "Lucille Sakbodin. She lives right over here on East Lincoln."

Amy and Leah walked slowly, slowly up East Lincoln. "There it is!" said Amy. She pointed to a large white car parked in a driveway.

"Are you sure?" said Leah. "After what you've told me, this whole thing is giving me the creeps."

Amy edged her way up the driveway.

"Where are you going?" Leah hissed.

"I want to take a closer look," said Amy. She crept nearer and nearer.

The front door flew open. "Taylor, where are you?" yelled Mrs. Sakbodin.

Amy dove under a bush.

"Taylor, is that you?" she said.

Amy held her breath.

A boy a couple of years older than Patrick

85

sauntered around from behind the house. "What do you want, Mom?" he said.

Amy stared. The boy had sandy blonde hair and a medium build. Taylor Sakbodin. *T.S.* Could this be the boy whom the man at the tractor shed described? The same boy who carved his initials in the bench?

"Would you run to town for me and pick up a newspaper?" said his mother. "I forgot to get one while I was there."

The boy made a face. "Now?"

"Take my car," said his mother.

It was at that moment that Amy noticed Leah, hiding underneath Mrs. Sakbodin's car. She must have started to follow Amy up the driveway, and when Mrs. Sakbodin came outside she'd ducked into the closest hiding place.

Amy signaled to her frantically.

Leah nodded and started to slither toward the edge of the driveway.

"Where did you leave the keys?" said Taylor.

"In my purse," said his mother. "In the kitchen." She followed her son inside.

The minute the door closed, Amy jumped up and ran over to Leah. "Are you okay?" she said.

Leah was pale. "Why do you get me into

these things?'' she groaned. ''You know how I hate danger.''

''Sorry,'' said Amy. ''I really am.'' She stared at the Sakbodin's house. ''Why do you think they fixed up the diamond?''

Leah brushed herself off. ''How should I know?''

''It doesn't make sense,'' said Amy. She got up and headed toward home. It seemed like every time she solved one thing, something else came up.

Back at her house, Amy tried to think things through again. Maybe the Sakbodins were baseball fans. Or maybe they were friends of Mrs. Allison, helping her out. Amy thought about Mrs. Sakbodin again and shook her head. Mrs. Sakbodin definitely didn't look like the helpful type.

The phone rang. ''I'll get it,'' said Amy.

It was her mother. ''I'm going to be late for dinner,'' she said. ''Would you do me a favor and cook up some more of those frozen chicken nuggets? You can put them in the microwave.''

''Okay,'' said Amy. ''What else are we having?''

''How about french fries and applesauce?'' said her mother. Mrs. Evans wasn't big on cooking. ''Is everything okay there?''

"Fine," said Amy. She suddenly remembered something. "Could you bring home the listing for the vacant lot I asked you about?"

"Sure," said her mother. "Where is the lot again?"

"On the corner of Pierce and Tyler," said Amy. Another thought occurred to her. "Could I have the listing for the lot on the corner of Hayes and Polk, too?"

"Will do," said her mother. "What do you want these for, anyway?"

"Nothing important," said Amy, brushing her off. "I'm just researching a story. See you later, Mom. Don't worry about dinner." She quickly hung up.

Amy was already in bed when her mother finally got home. "Hi, honey," she said, poking her head inside the door.

"Oh, hi," said Amy. "Long day, huh?"

"Very long," said her mother. "Here's those listings you wanted."

"Thanks, Mom," said Amy. "Good night."

"Good night," said her mother.

Amy leaned back on the pillow and studied the listings. There didn't seem to be anything special about either one. Both lots were about the same size, same everything except that the one on Hayes and Polk had recently raised its price, just as Mrs. MacKay had said.

Amy picked up the sheet with Mrs. Allison's lot again. Down in the corner it said, "Owner: Mrs. Harold Allison." Amy glanced at the other sheet. "What!" she said, sitting up in bed. "It can't be!" Written next to the word "owner" was a name Amy had never expected to find. Mrs. Lucille T. Sakbodin!

Chapter Seven

Amy sat on one of Vicky's purple cushions, drinking papaya juice and eating blue taco chips. Vicky always kept strange food around the house. Across the room, Vicky was studying the listings that Amy's mother had given her the night before.

"Verrrry interesting," said Vicky. "Do you understand what's going on?"

"I'm not sure," said Amy. "I keep thinking about that guy from Burger Boy. He felt bad when we told him how popular the diamond was." She thought for a minute. "Hey, wait! I got it! That was the whole point, to make Burger Boy feel bad. Mrs. Sakbodin figured that if she improved Mrs. Allison's lot enough, the kids would get involved in it and put up a fight about having it sold."

Vicky nodded. "Which was exactly what happened. And not only that," she said, "but she was so sure her little plan would work, that she raised the price on *her* lot, even though the location wasn't as nice. What a rat. She knew that a company as big as Burger Boy would probably pay the extra money for her lot rather than risk the bad publicity they'd get for kicking a bunch of innocent kids off the other one."

"That's really sneaky," said Amy.

"Very," said Vicky. "Have some more taco chips."

They crunched in silence for a few minutes.

"Now what?" said Amy.

Vicky looked at her. "Well, you're going to have to make a few decisions."

"Do we or don't we tell Burger Boy," said Amy.

"That's about the long and short of it," said Vicky.

"What would *you* do?" said Amy.

"I'd tell," said Vicky. "No question."

"Me too," said Amy. "Mrs. Sakbodin shouldn't be allowed to get away with this."

"I think you should be prepared, though," Vicky said, "for the possibility that Burger

Boy will still want to buy your lot, especially when they find out there's been some foul play."

One of Vicky's cats hopped onto Amy's lap and tried to chew on her taco chip.

"No, Horace," said Vicky. "You're supposed to be on a diet."

Amy moved the chip out of Horace's reach. "There's something else I wanted to ask you about," she said.

"Go ahead," said Vicky.

"It's about our neighbors, the Caspers." Amy explained how Robin had found out that the Caspers were one of the needy families and how she and Robin had asked Mrs. Casper if she'd be interested in being interviewed. "She got really mad at us," said Amy. She then went on to explain how she and Robin disagreed on whether or not the story should be written.

Vicky nodded. "I think your instincts were correct," she said. "There's something in newspaper lingo that we call 'the right to privacy.' It means that if people choose to keep information to themselves, they have that right as long as the information isn't hurting others." Vicky went on. "I can understand how you'd like to be able to help this family, especially since they're your neighbors. But if they don't want any help, and especially if they don't want to publicize their predicament, you should respect that. It's probably very embarrassing for Mrs. Casper not to be able to provide for her family. The last thing she wants to do is let everyone else know about it."

"That's what I thought," said Amy. "Maybe we should apologize to Mrs. Casper."

"I think Mrs. Casper would be just as happy if you dropped it," said Vicky. She smiled. "It's not always easy to be the editor, is it?"

"No," said Amy. She wished she didn't have to go back to face Erin and Robin. Neither one of them was going to be happy with what she had to tell them. "Do you want to come with me?"

"I don't think so." Vicky smiled. "I'm only the advisor."

"But maybe they'd listen to you," said Amy.

"Maybe they would," said Vicky, "but it's not my job. It's yours."

Amy took one last taco chip for the road. "Okay," she said, getting up from the floor.

Vicky showed her to the door. "Tell me how it goes," she said. "Promise?"

"Promise," said Amy.

* * *

"She *what?*" said Robin, lurching forward on the sofa.

Amy patiently explained the whole story about Mrs. Sakbodin one more time to everyone assembled in the treehouse.

Just as Amy had predicted, Erin gave her a suspicious look. "Are you sure you aren't making this whole thing up?" she said. "It sounds like a movie I once saw on TV."

"Maybe that's where Mrs. Sakbodin got the idea," said Leah. "Wait till you see her. She looks like a creepy vampire."

Robin poured half a box of little cinnamon hearts down her throat. "We're going to write a story about this, aren't we?"

"Well," said Amy, "we could. The only thing is, if we do, Burger Boy will probably decide to buy our lot. According to Vicky, it's the better buy."

"No way," said Erin. She shook her head and folded her arms.

"Erin," said Robin. "Don't you want fame and fortune?"

"Fame and fortune?" said Leah.

Robin grinned. "Sure," she said. "When everyone reads about how we exposed Mrs. Sakbodin, we'll be famous!"

Erin gave her a chilly stare. "I hardly think that's a good reason."

"Me neither," said Amy. "The reason we

should tell should be because Mrs. Sakbodin did something dishonest. People—especially the Burger Boy people—have the right to know."

"She used people," said Leah. "What a slime."

"But so what?" said Erin. "Look at all the good things that have happened since the diamond was improved. The neighbors have gotten together to sponsor teams, more and more kids are playing on the lot instead of out getting into trouble. I think we should keep our mouths shut."

"She has a point," said Robin. "Lots of kids go over there after school to play kickball now, not just the jocks."

"But the lot's going to sell eventually anyway, right?" said Amy. "No matter how you look at it, we lose."

"Not if we can convince Mrs. Allison to take it off the market," said Erin.

"She'll never do that," said Amy. "She needs the money. Besides, the point is that somebody has done something wrong. Mrs. Sakbodin shouldn't be allowed to get away with this."

"Can we write the story and not tell Burger Boy?" said Erin.

"They're going to find out eventually if we print the story," said Amy.

Erin tapped her knees together and stared out the window. "I think we should vote on it."

"Okay," said Amy. "I guess that's fair. There's something else first, though." She glanced at Robin. "It's about the Caspers."

"What about them?" said Robin.

Amy explained what Vicky had told her about people's right to privacy.

"So you definitely don't want to write a story?" said Robin.

"No," said Amy. "And I don't think we should tell anybody what we found out, either. It's our secret."

Robin slowly unwrapped a caramel chewie and stuck it in her mouth. She chewed it up and down and back and forth for a long time. "I'm not too happy about this," she said finally.

Amy swallowed. "I'm sorry."

"You know," said Leah. "It's sort of funny—we're really saying the opposite thing about these two stories."

"What do you mean?" asked Robin.

"Well, in the Casper's case, their right to privacy is being violated if we write the story, right?"

"Right," said Robin. "Even though we could help them."

"But in Mrs. Sakbodin's case," Leah continued, "we *want* to violate her privacy."

"Even though we could save the lot by keeping our mouths shut," said Erin.

"That's right," Amy said, remembering what Vicky had said. "Mrs. Sakbodin doesn't have the right to privacy, because what she's doing is hurting others."

"Let's vote on Mrs. Sakbodin," said Erin, not wasting any time. "All in favor of writing the story, raise your hand."

Only Amy and Leah's hands went up. Naturally.

Amy stared at Erin. Erin had always agreed with her on everything. Until now.

"Now what do we do?" said Leah.

"You can't write the story unless there's a majority," said Erin, as if Amy didn't know.

Amy got up from her chair. She had always felt that she tried to be fair with everyone. She wasn't going to make this any different. "I guess," she said, "that since we don't have a majority, we can't do anything. Meeting adjourned."

"Is that it?" said Robin. Amy could see she was itching for a big fight.

"That's it for now," said Amy firmly. "Until you or Erin change your mind."

"Never," said Erin.

"Okay," said Amy, pursing her lips. "Then

97

I guess I'll see you guys tonight at the party." She opened the hatch in the treehouse floor and climbed down the ladder. She wasn't feeling in much of a party mood.

She still wasn't hours later, with Robin's party in full swing down in her family room. Robin had turned the lights very low and had the stereo blasting away. There were baskets and baskets of chips, pretzels, and popcorn, and in the corner, a cooler full of soda. Most of the girls, including Amy, were standing in a little bunch over by the soda cooler. Most of the boys, led by Matt O'Connor, were trying to see who could shoot the most popcorn kernels into the cooler from across the room.

Amy had decided that she was going to pretend there was nothing the matter between her and Erin, even though Erin was obviously ignoring her.

"Hey, look out," shouted Daniel Metzler. A flying popcorn kernel hit Robin on the cheek.

"Ow!" said Robin. "Do you mind?"

The boys all hooted.

Amy tugged on her new sweater. She'd much rather have been at a slumber party. She glanced over at Erin, who had on a new pair of jeans. Erin must be dying about Matt being here. Amy wished she could talk with her about it.

Just then Lark Hogan walked right up to the middle of the boys and started talking to them, especially to Matt. Lark was the most beautiful girl in the sixth grade, head cheerleader, and totally stuck on herself. Amy was surprised Robin had invited her, since Robin didn't really like her. She *was* popular, though, and Robin had tried very hard to get all the popular kids to come to her party.

"What a flirt," said Danielle, watching Lark.

"Her socks are the wrong color," Robin observed. "No one wears socks that color."

Lark laughed at something Matt said.

Amy snuck a peek at Erin, who looked really miserable.

Robin's mother showed up. "Hi, kids," she said, looking around to make sure nobody was making out or getting into trouble.

"Don't worry, Mom," said Robin. "We're being good."

Robin's mother nodded and headed back upstairs. As soon as she did, Lark and Matt got into this sort of tickling game and Lark pretended to be mad even though everyone could see she wasn't.

"Somebody's going to be upset," Leah said under her breath.

Erin's face was turning redder and redder.

Amy reached over and grabbed a soda from the cooler. Right now Erin needed a friend. "What position am I playing tomorrow?" she asked as she handed Erin the soda.

Erin gave her a distracted look. "What did you say?"

"I said, what position am I playing tomorrow?"

Erin stared in the direction of Lark and Matt. "Now I know why Lark signed up for Matt's team," she said unhappily.

"But that's good," said Amy.

Erin gave her an uncomprehending look. "Why?"

"Because," said Amy, "now we have a good reason to beat them."

The next day, Erin stood on the pitcher's mound, concentrating on her next pitch. It was the top of the fifth, and the Treehouse Terrors had made it to the finals with the Brave Bulls, Matt's team. Amy was glad Erin had the brains to fill the rest of their team with good players. The other two teams, the Devil Dogs and the River Rats, sat on the sidelines watching. The pressure was starting to get to people.

From her position between first and second base, Amy surveyed the situation. There'd been a great turnout for the game. Behind the backstop, a load of groceries was piled four feet high, and between third and home, a crowd of spectators had been gathered since nine that morning, when the first game had been played. "Go, Terrors," shouted someone from the crowd. Probably one of Robin's sisters.

Amy kept her eye on Erin and tried to stay interested. All of the Treehouse Terrors had been given baggy brown T-shirts to wear over their jackets. Leah had decorated them herself with glittery leaves and little pizzas. They looked terrific.

Kim Phelan came up to kick.

"Easy out," yelled Robin from the outfield. Kim was Lark's best friend.

Erin pitched the ball and Kim gave a measly little kick. She didn't even make it halfway to first.

"Who's next?" shouted Robin.

Lark strolled up.

Erin bit her lower lip and pitched. The only other time Lark had been up, she'd made it all the way back to home.

"Ball one!" shouted the umpire.

Erin's next pitch was perfect. Lark kicked a grounder right toward Erin, who caught it and then ran over and shoved the ball

101

against Lark's back. "You're out!" she yelled triumphantly.

"Ow!" Lark rubbed her back, even though Erin hadn't hit her all that hard. "You don't have to be so rough, Erin," she whined.

Erin turned around and grinned at the others. "Who's next?" she said.

"Me," said Daniel.

Erin must have enjoyed getting her revenge, because for the next three innings she played like she belonged in a national kickball league. She even managed to score two home runs, which put the Terrors ahead by one.

By the top of the ninth, Erin looked pretty confident about winning. But then both Matt and Daniel scored home runs, putting the Brave Bulls ahead again by one run.

The Treehouse Terrors had one last inning to try to score. "What's the lineup?" said Erin.

"Leah, Robin, and me," said Amy glumly. "Your worst players."

"Don't say that," said Erin. "We're counting on you."

Leah gingerly stepped up to home plate. She had on a pair of hot pink high-topped sneakers, which made her feet look enormous. Unbelievably, she made it almost to second on an error before she was tagged out.

Robin was up next. Even though she slammed the ball over beyond third, Matt easily caught it and threw it to first before she got there.

Amy groaned. Two outs, no runs, and now it was her turn.

"We're counting on you," Erin repeated.

"I wish you wouldn't keep saying that," said Amy.

Daniel shot the ball toward her and she kicked. It went flying up in the air.

"Run," screamed Erin.

Amy took off. She watched as Matt ran toward the ball. Don't, please don't, she thought.

"You're out!" Matt yelled, catching the ball easily.

The Brave Bulls let out a cheer. "We win!" said Lark. "We win!"

Amy felt terrible. She'd blown the whole game. She'd known she was going to blow it, too. Why did Erin make her play, anyway? She walked back over to Erin and the rest of the team, who were huddled together behind home. "Sorry, guys," she said.

"That's okay," said Erin, who didn't look like she thought it was okay. "It's just a game."

103

The crowd had begun to break up. Several people came over to thank Erin and the rest of them for organizing everything.

"Look who's here," said Leah.

Mrs. Allison floated toward them wearing a long purple poncho. "What a lovely idea," she said, motioning to the poster about the tournament.

"We hope you didn't mind," said Erin.

"Oh no. Of course not." She gazed over at her For Sale sign. "I'm just sorry all of this is going to have to end."

Erin's eyes popped wide. "What?" she said.

"Why, yes," said Mrs. Allison. "I've had an offer for the property. Not nearly what I'd hoped, but one can't be too choosey."

The girls glanced at one another.

"Was it . . . Burger Boy?" said Robin.

"No, no," said Mrs. Allison. "Do you know the Salancey family? Dr. Salancey is a dentist. I believe he'd like to build an office here." She blotted her lips with a tissue. "Oh, look. There's Dotty Davis. Yoo hoo, Dotty." She wandered off.

Erin gazed sadly around the diamond. "A *dentist's* office?" she said.

Amy said, "Erin, I tried to warn you."

Erin looked away.

Robin popped a caramel chewie into her

104

mouth. "Personally, if I had a choice," she said, "I'd rather see it become a Burger Boy. Wouldn't you guys?"

"Does that mean you're changing your vote?" said Leah.

"I guess it does," said Robin.

Erin shook her head. She looked like she was about to cry.

"Erin, is that okay with you?" said Amy.

Erin sighed. "I guess it doesn't really make much difference, does it?"

Chapter Eight

Amy sat down at her desk in the treehouse, put on her favorite pair of blue angora gloves, and began typing. She started with her headline: "Foul Play Discovered on Ball Diamond." Now for the story. "Kirkridge residents will be angry to find out that something fishy has been happening in our neighborhood, thanks to one person."

Amy tapped her fingers against her glasses. She'd been thinking a lot about the diamond the past few days, about what Erin had said. The diamond *had* become important to many people, and it was too bad that it was going to disappear. She bent back over the keyboard. "It all started when the lot was put up for sale a few weeks ago by its owner, Mrs. Harold Allison," she typed.

"Hi," said Erin, quietly climbing through the hatch. "Am I bothering you?"

"No," said Amy. "I'm just waiting for everyone else to show up." She paused. "I started the story about the diamond."

Erin nodded. "How can you type with gloves on?"

"I only use two fingers," said Amy. An uncomfortable silence passed. "I'm sorry the diamond is going to be sold," Amy said finally.

Erin stared at the floor. "Me too."

"And I'm sorry I lost the game for us," said Amy.

"That's okay," said Erin. "At least I got Lark out." She sat down on the sofa. "I guess I've been acting like a baby, huh?"

"It's not your fault," said Amy. "It's Mrs. Sakbodin's fault. She's the one we should be mad at."

"I know," said Erin. "I finally figured that out."

They were suddenly interrupted by Robin, who struggled through the hatch saying, "Ohmygosh. You aren't going to believe this." Right behind her was Leah.

"What is it?" said Amy.

"First of all, I saw her," said Robin.

107

"Saw who?" said Erin.

"Mrs. Sakbodin," said Robin. "I knew it was her because of the armadoodle."

"The what?" said Leah.

"The armadoodle," said Robin. "It looked like a dachshund with scales."

"Oh," said Leah.

"I think you mean arma*dillo,* Robin," said Erin.

"Thank you, Erin," Robin said sarcastically.

"Where was she?" interrupted Amy.

"In our shoe store," said Robin. "I've never seen her in there before. That's not what I wanted to tell you, though. I found out something even better."

"What?" said Amy. By now, they had all clustered themselves around Robin, who had seated herself on the sofa.

"You guys are going to be so proud of me," she said.

"What *is* it?" said Erin.

"Well," said Robin, "I wanted to be sure it was her, okay? So when I saw that she was probably going to buy something, I decided to hang around to see how she was going to pay. Most people who buy shoes use credit cards or checks," she explained.

"Which have their names on them," Amy added.

"Obviously," said Robin. She stopped long enough to pop a caramel chewie. "I waited a long time. She was very picky. Finally she bought a pair of red high heels, the tall kind that squish your toes. She paid with a check. After she left, I went over to the register and looked at her name. Lucille T. Sakbodin. That's when I made my big discovery." She looked at the others. "Are you ready? As I was studying her check, I noticed something weird about her handwriting." She paused. "Does no capital letters ring a bell?"

Amy gasped.

"The letter to the editor!" said Erin.

"That's right," said Robin. "I'm sure it was her." She stood up and bowed with a flourish. "Thank you, thank you. It was nothing."

"What a sneak," said Erin, "Telling us we should start a league!"

"That was good investigating, Robin," said Amy. She shook her head. Not only had Mrs. Sakbodin used the kids in the neighborhood, she'd used the *Treehouse Times,* too.

Erin walked over to the typewriter. "You've started your story already, right?"

Amy nodded.

"Good," said Erin. "Because I want to help."

"Me too," said Robin. "I want everyone in the whole world to know what a greaseball Mrs. Lucille T. Sakbodin is."

The next morning, Amy was bent over her kitchen table, checking the final layout of their Thanksgiving issue. At the top right of the first page was the story about Mrs. Sakbodin. Underneath that was the story about the food drive, with Leah's funny illustrations. The next two pages included the story about the charity tournament, Erin's poll, and the other monthly features.

"You must be very proud of yourselves," said her mother, coming up behind her. "You did some great detective work."

Amy grinned and took one last gulp of her orange juice. "Thanks, Mom," she said. "It was worth it." As soon as she'd finished writing her story about Mrs. Sakbodin yesterday, Amy had showed it to her mother, who couldn't believe what Mrs. Sakbodin was up to. Her mother had called Mrs. MacKay, who called the realty board, who called up Mrs. Sakbodin. Boy, was she in trouble! Mrs. Allison had found out, too, and said she decided not to sell to Dr. Salancey yet. Amy guessed she was holding out for Burger Boy.

"Remember to get Mr. Werner's address

for me today," Amy said to her mother. "We decided to send him a copy of the paper."

"I'll bring it home tonight," said Mrs. Evans.

Amy's father came into the kitchen. "Have you got that paper ready for me?" he asked, while tying his necktie.

"Here it is," said Amy.

Mr. Evans looked it over. "Nice job, honey," he said. "You've turned into a real crusader, haven't you?"

Amy smiled and watched as her father carefully put the layout into his briefcase.

"Kind of like watching a child go off to school for the first time, isn't it?" he observed.

"What's that supposed to mean?" said Amy.

"Oh, I don't know. It has to do with letting go of something which you've spent a long time nurturing."

"Yeah," said Amy slowly. "I guess you're right."

After Thanksgiving, interest in the lot seemed to die down, although Amy always checked to see if the For Sale sign was still there whenever she passed the lot. People were more into Christmas than kickball, and it was getting too cold to play outdoors anyway. Even with the *Treehouse Times*'s scoop, Amy was afraid that by the time warm weather came around, everybody would have forgotten. She'd almost forgotten herself until one December Saturday when she picked up the ringing phone.

"Amy, this is Nathan Werner from Burger Boy," the voice on the other end said.

Amy swallowed the carrot she had just snitched out of the salad she was helping her father make. "Hi," she said.

"Amy, I've been meaning to call to thank you for bringing the matter of the kickball diamond to our attention," he began.

"You're welcome," said Amy.

Mr. Werner cleared his throat. "I have some news for you which I thought you might find interesting."

"You've decided to buy the lot," said Amy sadly.

"We have," said Mr. Werner. "But we know how much everyone has enjoyed the diamond and Burger Boy wants to see activities like these encouraged."

Amy wondered where the conversation was leading.

"Are you familiar with the vacant lot across from the diamond?" said Mr. Werner.

"You mean the one with the shed?" said Amy.

112

"That's right," said Mr. Werner. "It's too small for us to build a restaurant on, but we think it would make a great diamond."

"But there's a shed on it," said Amy. "With a tractor."

Mr. Werner laughed. "I guess I didn't make myself clear. Burger Boy has just bought that lot from the gas station owner. We're going to tear down the shed and put up a diamond for you."

Amy gasped.

"Amy? You still there?"

"Yes," said Amy, pinching herself. "I think I'm still here."

"We want to thank you again for alerting us to the situation," said Mr. Werner.

"Oh," said Amy, still in a daze. "It was nothing." It was a dumb response, but she just wanted to get off the phone so she could call Erin.

"I'll be calling you again in a few weeks to let you know our plans," he said. "So you can write it up in that terrific paper of yours."

"Uh, okay," said Amy. "Thank you. Thank you very much." She hung up.

"Good news?" asked Mr. Evans, as if he couldn't tell from the expression on Amy's face.

"Fantastic!" said Amy. "Burger Boy

bought that little lot across the street from the diamond and they're going to build us a new diamond!"

"You're kidding!" said her father. "That's great!"

"I know," said Amy. She picked up the phone again. "Hi, Erin?" she said. "Guess what! I've got unbelievable news!"

MEET THE GIRLS FROM CABIN SIX IN

Coming Soon

CAMP SUNNYSIDE FRIENDS #5
LOOKING FOR TROUBLE

75909-8 ($2.50 US/$2.95 Can)

When the older girls at camp ask Erin to join them in some slightly-against-the-rules escapades, she has to choose between appearing cool and being mature.

Don't Miss These Other
Camp Sunnyside Adventures:

(#4) NEW GIRL IN CABIN SIX

75703-6 ($2.50 US/$2.95 Can)

(#3) COLOR WAR! 75702-8 ($2.50 US/$2.95 Can)

(#2) CABIN SIX PLAYS CUPID

75701-X ($2.50 US/$2.95 Can)

(#1) NO BOYS ALLOWED! 75700-1 ($2.50 US/$2.95 Can)